Th

Crop Circles
Appear
Overnight

BUSLOADS OF
CURIOUS TOURISTS
BOOST ECONOMY—
ALIENS ARE GREAT!
SAYS CHAMBER OF
COMMERCE

I WAS MARRIED TO AN ALIEN

And most
shocking
of all...

GORGEOUS SINGLE MAN ARRIVES IN TOWN

—Now, that's a story worth pursuing,
knows reporter Ciel Landry

Dear Reader,

Mother knows best—maybe! That's the theme of our miniseries Matchmaking Mothers (from Hell). Ruth Jean Dale launches this fun series with *A Royal Pain*.

I think we can all relate to meddling mothers, only these matchmaking moms take events to the extreme. How is a respectable woman to become a grandmother unless her offspring cooperates? There's nothing to be done except to get the kids down the aisle, even if they go kicking and screaming all the way! Plans are made, schemes hatched, plots unraveled.

Next month the miniseries continues with Vicki Lewis Thompson's *One Mom Too Many*. Watch for more Matchmaking Mothers (from Hell) in the months ahead!

Not to be outdone in amusement is Suzannah Davis's *Heatcrazed!* An entire town goes a little crazy during a heat wave, and the "invasion" of laughter begins. Suzannah is a longtime popular author familiar to romance readers. She's also a great fan of "Star Trek" and "The X-Files," as I think you'll be able to tell from her delightfully comic take on Fox Mulder's favorite obsession. Enjoy!

With love and laughter,

Malle Vallik

Malle Vallik
Associate Senior Editor

HEATCRAZED!
Suzannah Davis

Harlequin Books

TORONTO • NEW YORK • LONDON
AMSTERDAM • PARIS • SYDNEY • HAMBURG
STOCKHOLM • ATHENS • TOKYO • MILAN
MADRID • WARSAW • BUDAPEST • AUCKLAND

ISBN 0-373-44016-2

HEATCRAZED!

This edition published by arrangement with Harlequin Books S.A.

® and TM are trademarks of the publisher. Trademarks indicated with ® are registered in the United States Patent and Trademark Office, the Canadian Trade Marks Office and in other countries.

Printed in U.S.A.

Growing up with a Jupiter-sized crush on Captain Kirk, a Southerner's fancy and the certainty that fairies lived in my garden, is it any wonder I've always looked into the night sky and thought, *What if?*

My family is known for deep philosophical debates over the Force and whether Wookies have fleas, so alien visitations are a "hot" topic at my house—and not just during the dog days of summer. Unfortunately, however, I've never been taken on a wild spaceship ride (no matter how hard I wished). That's why *Heatcrazed!* was so much fun to write. So indulge in the possibilities even if your friends think you're moonstruck—and may all your close encounters fill the universe with love and laughter.

—Suzannah Davis

To Brian, Jill and Brad—
May you always reach for the stars!

1

"AM I WRONG, or has everyone around here gone completely looney-tunes?"

With a weary sigh, Ciel Landry dropped the latest edition of the *Whiskey Bay Press* into her mother's lap and flopped down in a folding lawn chair next to her.

"You've got to expect a few cases of insanity when the August dog days hit," Marie Landry said with a laugh. *"Especially in Whiskey Bay."*

Although it was after eight in the evening, rays from the burning Louisiana sun still streamed through the branches of the towering, ancient oaks shading the backyard of the Landrys' home. Thanks to the Southern one-two punch of killer humidity and high temperature, the heat index was well over the 100-degree mark. Ciel swept her shoulder-length strawberry ringlets back from her flushed face. With an apologetic grin, she seized hold of her mother's tall glass of iced tea and gulped down the contents.

"A few cases?" Ciel pressed the cool glass to her forehead and sighed again. "It's more like a major epidemic. Since yesterday, Sally Jessup's called the sheriff out three times about burglars on her roof with flashlights, and they caught eighty-two-year-old Adelaide Posner on the interstate doing 110."

Marie considered Ciel's comment as she smoothed the

tidy skirt and gingham blouse she'd worn to her secre-
tarial job at the church rectory.

Whiskey Bay's citizens—a mixture of Cajun, French
Creole, African American and redneck with a touch of
gator thrown in—clung to their way of life and traditions
as tenaciously as the gray Spanish moss that clung to
the oak trees. The town's eccentrics were a source of
pride—at least most of the time. And the Landry family
had their share, Marie had to admit.

"Adelaide told me she just wanted to see how fast
that old DeSoto would go," Marie explained with a sly
grin on her face.

"And Lincoln Dobbs? What possessed him to strip
buck naked and sunbathe on top of the bank building?"

"Poor circulation?" Marie's brown eyes danced with
mischief. "And I guess you heard Nap Conly tied one
on this afternoon and drove his new Ford pickup into
Judge Taylor's swimming pool."

"You're kidding."

Marie pointed to the portable telephone in the grass
next to her chair. "Your Aunt Tee-Ta called just ten
minutes ago."

Ciel grinned. Marie's extensive communications net-
work of friends and relatives put CNN to shame, which
wasn't a bad thing for a reporter living under the same
roof. The daily papers out of Lafayette and Baton Rouge
took care of national and state news, but the *Press* had
the scoop on what people around Whiskey Bay *really*
wanted to know.

Unfortunately, in recent months Mr. Crenshaw, the
absentee owner, had been looking for any excuse to
close the doors of his borderline profitable *Press*. Ciel's
fast talking and drastic cost cutting had held him off so

far. But for how long? In a town with only two thousand souls and few opportunities, she needed the job.

"Well, a story on Nap's mishap makes more interesting reading than what our illustrious mayor has to say," Ciel said.

Marie snorted. "That ignoramus! Emile Nabors is more interested in protecting his job than improving our town. Why, I could run things better hogtied and blindfolded."

"At least Emile isn't wandering around in his birthday suit! I swear I'm beginning to think there's something in the water. Anything else I should know about?"

"Well, Tee-Ta saw a strange man in the Piggly-Wiggly today. Hardly said a word, but real easy on the eyes. Had all the checkout girls in a swoon. She thought maybe since you and Izzy aren't seeing each other anymore..."

"Mama!" Ciel's voice carried a warning.

"I'm merely passing on the message. You want your supper now?"

Grateful for the change of subject, Ciel shook her head. "I'm too hot. The air-conditioning in my car quit again, and I had to make the run to the printing plant in Crowley. But we got the papers addressed and delivered to the post office, so everything's under control—at least until next week's issue."

"That Roy Crenshaw works you too hard, *chère*." Marie pursed her lips, and her salt-and-pepper curls quivered as she shook her head in disapproval. "It's a disgrace to treat his editor in chief that way!"

"It feels more like idiot in chief lately," Ciel muttered ruefully. "Where's Kyle?" Twelve-year-old Kyle, the baby of the family, was at that age when he was forever getting into one scrap or another, and Ciel worried about

what he was up to, wondering if he, too, had been in-
fected with late-summer madness.

Marie shrugged and rose to her feet. "He and Tony
are around somewhere. You know those boys in the
summer—fishing, swimming, God knows what else.
Why don't you stay here and cool off while I make some
more iced tea?"

The warped screen porch door whacked shut behind
Marie, and Ciel settled back into her chair in a loose-
limbed slouch. The kinks in her tired neck had barely
begun to ease, when Kyle and his perpetual shadow, his
eleven-year-old cousin, Tony Pearson, burst through the
bushes at the edge of the yard. The two boys skidded to
a stop at her feet.

"Ciel! Ya gotta see!" Wide-eyed and gasping, Kyle
Landry swept his long, brown hair back from his tanned
forehead. "It's too weird!"

"Yeah, Ciel, ya gotta!" Tony echoed. Clad in identical oversized T-shirts and frayed cutoffs, the brown-
eyed cousins were closer than brothers and as insepa-
rable as Siamese twins. "Come on!"

Ciel groaned. "Not now, fellows. The crazies have
been howling at the moon all week, and I'm not in the
mood to discuss intergalactic philosophy with two space
cadets."

"But it's Uncle Etienne's camp," Kyle insisted. "It's
all locked up, and we had to climb the fence, and I
dropped my pole, and...and you're a reporter, aren't
you?"

"Yes, but—why, you boys are both white as sheets!"
Ciel sat up, scowling. Nothing much rattled youngsters
who wandered the bayous as freely as these did, but they
were both breathing hard, agitated, almost panicked.
"You say the gate was locked?"

"And they even hung a chain over the end of the dock!" Tony's tone was aggrieved.

"That's odd. Uncle Etienne never minded if anyone used his place before."

The Etienne Ballard camp, located on the water a scant mile through the palmetto-and-scrub-oak woods from the Landrys' back door, had always been considered home-away-from-home territory, even after the old man, a longtime friend of the Landrys, had moved into the local nursing home. But the camp was fairly isolated. What if the boys had stumbled onto something nefarious, something illegal?

Ciel's head filled with visions of gangster types with automatic weapons and secret caches of smuggled drugs. The part of her that longed for adventure and regretted giving up the investigative reporter beat in Atlanta prodded her to action. If something *was* going on at the Ballard place, wasn't it her moral and civic duty to discover what?

"Maybe I *had* better take a look...."

Moments later, Ciel was being pulled along the well-beaten path through the overgrown thicket by two overexcited youngsters and trying not to stumble over her feet in the fading light. Palmetto fronds slapped her ankles and a mosquito bit her behind her ear.

"You can quit dragging my skirt, Tony," she protested. "Honestly, what's wrong with you two?"

Kyle's teeth were actually chattering.

"Tell her, Tony."

"There's this big...in the back." Tony gulped noisily. "And it's got these *eyes*."

Monsters? Ciel groaned. "I swear, the heat's gotten to you, too. If this is another one of your tricks..."

"No, honest to God, cross my heart!" Kyle said. They

stumbled out of the thick undergrowth onto the weed-choked banks of a bayou bordered by tall cypress trees. Kyle crouched low and whispered. "You just—"

"I know—*gotta*." She sighed, unconsciously mimicking his tone and stance.

Through the haze of dusk they approached a weathered gray cypress-board camp house. It sat on the water like a squat toad, well back from the two-lane gravel main road out front. The building perched on thick pilings and was surrounded by the shadowy, faintly sinister bulk of dark railings and screened porches. No lights shone from within, but a tan van sat in the narrow drive. Behind the camp, a long, sturdy dock poked into the water.

Ciel tried to be philosophical. She'd always known these two had wild imaginations. She'd just humor the boys a bit longer. "Okay, where's this thing I gotta see?" she whispered.

Tony gestured, pushed through the bushes and led them across a lawn of foot-high grass until they could almost see directly onto the rear porch. "Around here. Be real careful. It's locked up, but it's big—big as Sasquatch, I reckon."

"Or Frankenstein," Kyle added.

Ciel got a case of goose bumps. "You're making my skin crawl."

"Yeah, well, wait till you see—shh!" Kyle grabbed Ciel's arm, and she jumped.

"What?"

"Darn! It's gone!"

"It was right there, I promise," Tony wailed softly. "You gotta believe us, Ciel."

"Come on, let's get a closer look. Maybe there's

some sign left.'' Kyle ran in a crouch toward the back porch steps leading to a wooden veranda.

''Kyle! Come back here!'' Ciel ordered furiously. She had taken a step to follow, when he gave a yelp and fell heavily to the earth. ''Kyle!''

All thought of stealth forgotten, Ciel charged across the grassy space in front of the steps, with Tony right on her heels. Kyle was rolling on the ground, clenching his shin.

''It bit me, Ciel! It bit me!''

''What? A snake?'' Cold terror knotted Ciel's belly. She went down on her knee beside Kyle, dragged him upright and reached for his sock. ''Let me see. Oh, my God!''

Kyle looked up, and his eyes shone white with fright. ''Watch out! Behind you!''

Tony hollered and grabbed Ciel's neck in a stranglehold. Kyle clutched her hands. Ciel lost her balance as she tried to swing around. She brushed something metallic, and caught a painful charge that jolted all three of them. With a trio of howls, they fell into a tangled heap, then screamed again in unison as a huge, ghost-white, bug-eyed apparition bore down upon them out of the gloom.

The phantom threw back the lapels of a white lab coat and ripped off a headset bulging with lenses.

''What the *hell's* going on out here?''

JOHN CHURCHILL ''Jack'' Cooper glowered at the pile of tangled humanity sprawled at his feet. He couldn't find badly needed solitude even in this isolated backwater of civilization! All he could make out of this human Gordian knot were assorted arms and legs and a wild shock of strawberry curls.

"Don't just stand there!" the woman on the bottom of the pile snapped. "Kyle's been snake bitten!"

"What!" Stringing his headset onto his arm, Jack squatted beside her, then realized that her two companions were both boys. "Where's the wound? Did he see the snake? Poisonous or nonpoisonous? How long ago?"

"I don't know what kind! It just happened. Kyle, let me *see*."

"I'm okay, Ciel—whoops!"

Jack scooped up the kid and stormed toward the cabin. "Come on. It's too dark out here to see a damn thing. Step over the hot wire."

"He needs a doctor," she said anxiously, scrambling up after them. "I'll call an ambulance. Is there a phone? Tony, come—*what hot wire?*"

Kyle, all arms and legs, was surprisingly solid. And slippery. "Mister, wait a minute—"

"Take it easy, kid," Jack ordered, kicking open the screen door.

He strode through the back porch and into the dark cabin, then found a switch with his elbow. Light flooded the rustic kitchen, with its enamel sink, open shelves and sturdy pine table. Vials and beakers filled with noxious-looking mixtures littered the cabinet tops, along with a forgotten bologna sandwich and a threadbare T-shirt Jack had stripped out of after unloading the van earlier. A wood-paneled sitting room was furnished with Herculon-upholstered chairs, and a sagging sofa lay beyond the kitchen. Boxes of files and stacks of reference books formed a scholarly clutter around a personal computer perched atop a rickety desk.

Jack plunked the boy onto the kitchen table. "Okay, where'd he hit you?"

"Nowhere. That is, I mean—" Red-faced, Kyle clutched his shin.

"Let's have a look." Jack peeled the boy's fingers away.

"Get your hands off my brother!"

Her words a furious hiss, the woman called "Ciel" shouldered Jack aside—quite a feat, since he was no lightweight and she barely reached his shoulder. But while she was delicately built, slender yet rounded in all the right places beneath her jumper, she was powerful enough in her agitation to push past Jack. He caught a whiff of something vaguely floral and feminine and a little salty, but he was too busy defending himself to analyze the way his belly clenched involuntarily at her nearness.

Ciel slapped at his hands. "I'll take care of this!"

"Don't get hysterical on me," Jack ordered, ignoring her attempts to loosen his hold on Kyle's leg. White-faced with strain, the boy she'd called "Tony" hovered beside a cabinet. "Hand me that shirt, son."

"What—this?" Tony held out the garment, whose faded logo commemorated the launch of a space shuttle mission.

"It'll do for a tourniquet," Jack muttered, with only fleeting regret at the sacrifice of his favorite shirt. "I hope Etienne has a snake bite kit around here somewhere—"

"It wasn't a snake!" Kyle yelled, exasperated.

His sister jumped. "But you said—"

"I must have brushed that electric fence," he admitted sheepishly.

"You're sure?" Jack rotated the boy's lower leg, examining every inch of skin for the telltale twin fang marks.

Nothing. Except a little dirt. Thank God.

Blowing out a deep, relieved breath, Jack unslung his headset from his arm and set it on the table with a resounding thump that probably did the sophisticated magnification system not one iota of good. "Well, why the devil didn't you say so?"

Kyle shrugged, as embarrassed as an adolescent could get. "I tried—"

"How could he think with you leaping dementedly out of the brush and scaring us all half to death?"

The woman's blue eyes flashed with temper as she charged to her brother's defense.

"I did not leap," Jack retorted. "I was merely examining some of the local flora and came to investigate the commotion."

She was too incensed to be pacified by such a meager excuse. "Whoever heard of such a thing—an electric fence, for God's sake! How dare you! How dare you booby-trap this place with such a nefarious instrument of torture? Against *unsuspecting children,* no less! You are the lowest, most vile, despicable—"

"That little wire has such a low voltage all it does is tingle," Jack protested.

"Ha! If you believe that, then you grab hold! It hurts!" She punched Jack's broad chest with her forefinger for emphasis.

"I'm just trying to keep the raccoons out of my algae."

Her eyes widened incredulously. "Your what?"

Jack made a sweeping gesture around the kitchen, including the screened porch, where rows of jars lined a wobbly redwood picnic table. "Algae. Aquatic nonvascular plant life. The raccoons like the sugar I'm feeding it."

"Way out!" Kyle said, impressed.

"Cool!" Tony echoed, still clutching the commemorative shirt.

Ciel eyed the beakers dubiously, then wrinkled her nose in disgust. "You mean *pond scum?*"

"Experimental hydroponic algoids for oxygen replenishment."

"Experiments?" she scoffed. "What are you, some kind of mad scientist or something?"

The redhead's scornful disdain of his work provoked Jack's choler in a manner he hadn't experienced in years of self-disciplined composure.

"I'm a biologist. And I'm not mad yet." His voice dropped ominously. *"But I'm getting there."*

She blushed, a bright peachy tide that flooded her skin from neckline to her enticing widow's peak. Undaunted, she lifted her chin and glared at him. "Just because you fancy yourself Louis Pasteur doesn't give you the right to go around terrorizing innocent people!"

"If you three had noticed the locked gate or obeyed the No Trespassing signs, none of this would have happened!" Jack shouted.

Ciel hesitated, her even teeth tugging at her lower lip in a fashion that Jack found highly unsettling.

"Well," she said at last, "you might have a point there. I guess you weren't to know no one around here would take something like that seriously, not after we've been using this place for simply *ages*. However, since you really were nice about Kyle's snake bite, I guess we can overlook it."

"*You* guess..." Jack opened his mouth, then closed it again, stupefied.

"It's the least we can do for a new neighbor." The feisty belligerence was gone, replaced by a quick, feminine appraisal that took in everything from his slightly too-long black hair to his shoe size. She either liked what she saw, or else had merely decided that he wasn't an ax murderer after all. She stuck out her hand. "I'm Ciel Landry, Mr.—"

"Cooper," he said through lips so tight they would have done Clint Eastwood proud. "Er, Jack Cooper."

Silently breathing a sigh of relief when that admission provoked no answering gleam of recognition in any of the three faces, Jack took her hand just long enough to appease Miss Manners, then released it.

"Well, I live about a mile back that way, Jack."

Ciel waved, then gave him a smile that lit up her pretty, freckled face like sunshine.

"Welcome to Whiskey Bay."

Stunned by the warmth of that smile, Jack sucked in a breath at the involuntary stirring of masculine interest. It was as surprising as it was unwelcome, for this woman was not at all his type. No, he liked sophisticated, intelligent women, women like his ex-wife, Retha, and certainly not a frizzle-haired, overly excitable smart aleck, even if she did possess the most amazing sapphire-colored eyes he'd ever seen. As quickly as the sensation had seized him, he forced it down again. The last thing he needed in his life right now was a ditzy redhead brewing trouble and diverting his attention from the reason he'd come to this outpost in the first place.

"Not from around here, are you?" she asked.

Jack frowned. "No."

"Plan on staying long?"

"Depends."

"Are you renting this place from Uncle Etienne?"

Somewhat amazed that she remained undaunted by his monosyllabic answers, Jack hesitated, then told the truth.

"Ah, his nephew, René, is a friend of mine. He's letting me borrow it."

"Oh, great! You'll love it here. Best fishing on the entire bayou. Best place to beat some of this insufferable summer heat, too, and maybe hang on to your sanity at the same time. Do you like to fish, Jack?"

Jack felt his ears growing red. He wasn't accustomed to getting the third degree from trespassers! Rolling onto the heels of his running shoes, he swept back his lab coat and stuck his palms into the back pockets of his faded jeans in his preferred showdown stance. His words were clipped.

"Fishing is not the issue here, Miss Landry. I'm a very busy man, and I've got a lot to accomplish and little time to do it. Unless you can explain why you've invaded my privacy, I really must ask you to leave now and not come back."

"Gosh, we're really sorry, mister." Kyle gulped hard and slid off the table. "We didn't mean any harm. I just thought—"

"Kyle left his spinning reel," Ciel interjected, cutting off her brother's explanations. "You don't object to *him* retrieving his property, do you?"

Jack groaned inwardly. Irritation made his voice sharper than he intended. "No, of course not. Although you might have knocked on the front door."

"Don't be silly," Ciel scoffed. "Lots of people have been passing through Ballard Road and using the dock for years—"

"I've noticed. Why else would I put up signs?"

She peered at him from underneath a flutter of thick lashes, her smile sweetly cajoling now.

"Well, you see, there's a kind of unwritten tradition around here about that. Now that you've met the boys—

Kyle, Tony, this is Mr. Cooper—surely you wouldn't mind if they continued to come fishing here, would you? They wouldn't be any bother.''

Jack gave the youngsters a wry glance. In his thirty-six years, he'd seen all kinds of trouble, but these two were pure menace in tennis shoes. His mouth twisted. ''Right.''

She had the grace to blush again.

''I assure you they're not always so…so impetuous as tonight.''

Jack wasn't in the mood to be cajoled, not even by a beguiling redhead, so his features remained as impassive as a cigar store Indian's. ''My privacy concerns me, Miss Landry. Trespassers will be prosecuted.''

Ciel blinked. ''You're joking!''

''I do not joke.''

''Yeah, well, you ought to have something done about that,'' she muttered.

Stiffening at her barb, Jack hooked a thumb in his belt loop, his expression stony. ''I'm quite serious about my solitude, Miss Landry. I suggest you don't test my resolve in this matter. I'll see you out.''

Ciel's blue eyes darkened with temper and her lush mouth firmed, but the glance she gave him was faintly pitying.

''Your mistake, Jack.'' Turning, she waved the boys toward the door. ''Come on, fellows. We've disturbed Mr. Cooper enough for one evening.''

''For sure,'' Kyle said fervently.

Tony passed the T-shirt back to Jack on his way out. ''Cool shirt, sir.''

Ciel paused at the door long enough to slant him a small half smile that was somehow more alarming for all its seeming warmth.

"See you around."

Not if I see you first, Jack thought with a grimace.

Then the back door slammed behind them, and the unlikely trio disappeared into the darkness. Jack felt as though he'd survived a three-day centrifuge ride—barely. Dazed, he sank onto a wooden kitchen chair and stared at the faint outline of the space shuttle *Columbia* still visible on the shirt. Shaking his head, he tossed the shirt aside and dragged both hands down his face.

He needed some sleep. Some hot food. And, by the way his libido jumped every time that infuriating redhead had come too close, a woman.

But Jack Cooper could control his urges, especially when the stakes were high, so he resolutely put everything out of his mind except his work. Because if he didn't pull his research together and turn in his grant proposal in six weeks' time, he wasn't going to spend next year researching in the Brazilian rain forest, nearly five years' work would go down the tubes and, worst of all, Retha—damn her!—would likely win the funding that he was counting on to continue his project.

Retha was as brilliant and as coolly logical as he was, a perfect choice in a mate for a man like him—or so he'd thought. The fact was, they'd spent more time in the two years of their marriage in the laboratory than in bed. Neither of them really seemed to care or even notice much when Retha had packed her bags and left for a juicy assistant professorship with her new flame, one of the top names in exobiology. The fact was, losing the data Retha had lifted when she'd left him four years ago had hurt almost as much as her leaving him for another man, and he damned well wasn't going to let his ex-wife use his own work to beat him out of this grant.

But lately it seemed as if all the cards were stacked

against him. Congress had red-lined last year's grant money; there had been a disastrous fire in the university lab he'd counted on using in Houston; and his graduate students had made so many demands on his time the previous semester he'd fallen seriously behind in his own research.

René Ballard, Jack's friend and mentor, sensing Jack's growing stress, had suggested his great-uncle Etienne's isolated Louisiana camp house. Desperate, Jack jumped at the offer, seeing a chance to pull himself together and get back on track. René had assured Jack that in Whiskey Bay he'd find all the peace and quiet he needed and then some. Jack exhaled deeply and shook his head. If René only knew!

Jack pictured the comical pile of terrified interlopers he'd discovered in his yard. He supposed that his flapping down on them out of the gloom, wearing that space-aged headset, must have been scary at that. In fact, he could truthfully say, Ciel Landry's stunned face had been quite something to see.

Jack's lips twitched. "Boo!" he said out loud, then began to laugh.

It had been so long since he'd laughed it sounded more like rusty hinges than real merriment, but Jack filled his lungs and laughed again, thinking about Ciel and her two cohorts. Crazy redhead. Tears of mirth moistened the corners of his eyes, and his sides ached.

It felt good. Damn good.

2

"DAMN MACHINE!"

Elbow-deep in the electronic guts of a cranky second-hand typesetting computer, Ciel cursed and thought longingly of the days of Linotypes, letter presses and molten lead. For the third time in two days, the gremlins had gone wild, effectively putting the *Press* out of business.

Defeated, Ciel shoved up the sleeves of her white shirt and glared at the bits and pieces of electronic hardware, maintenance manuals, snakelike electrical cords and assorted screws and covers that littered the work table.

"I give up! I don't know what the devil's wrong with this thing, Lauren!"

Petite and voluptuous Lauren Herbert jammed her manicured hands into the back pockets of her skintight jeans in annoyance.

"If Skinflint Crenshaw would spring for a new system," she said, pouting, "we wouldn't be in this fix every two seconds. I suppose I could use the Mac computer at the bank, but Tiny isn't going to like me having to work late again."

"I know. I'm sorry," Ciel said with a sigh.

"Tiny" Herbert, Lauren's six-four former-football-player husband wasn't the only one. Still, it didn't pay to antagonize a man that size, especially a newlywed so besotted with his brunette sexpot bride he had been known to crush an unopened can of Coors beer in one beefy hand when any other male got too close. Tiny tended his rice fields and crawfish ponds from daylight to dusk, and he couldn't be blamed for wanting his wife at home to greet him each evening, even if she was the fastest typist in south Louisiana and indispensable to Ciel. Since Lauren and Ciel and the handful of students and part-time help were all the "staff" there was, some-times—like now—just handling day-to-day operations at the small paper was a challenge.

"I just hate to complain to Crenshaw when he's look-ing for any excuse to shut us down, Lauren," Ciel said, picking up a snap-in circuit board for another try at the recalcitrant machine. "We might both be out of a job then."

"Yeah, I guess you're right." The expression on Lau-ren's heart-shaped face was doleful as she leaned against the wooden counter that separated the back of the shop from the customer service area out front.

Under banks of fluorescent lights, the rear work space was a jumble of drawing boards, layout books, typeset-ting equipment, scissors, T-squares and overflowing wastebaskets. On the wall opposite the front door, an assortment of brass-plated Louisiana Newspaper Asso-ciation award plaques lined the walls, along with a mis-cellany of political cartoons pinned up with thumbtacks, Ciel's diploma from the LSU School of Journalism and a yellow bumper sticker that read Beam Me Up, Scotty. There's No Intelligent Life Down Here.

As Lauren watched Ciel's efforts, her dark eyes took on a mischievous sparkle. "Too bad Izzy isn't as good with computers as he is with motors."

"Old news, Lauren," Ciel said, frowning as she tried to fit the computer circuit board back into its slot. From deep in the bowels of the building, the ancient air conditioner groaned and threatened to give up the fight altogether. "I told you Izzy Chaston and I aren't seeing each other anymore."

"That's not the way I hear Izzy tell it down at the Stop and Go Garage, darlin'," Lauren said, shooting her friend a sly look from under indecently long black lashes.

"Well, you hear wrong, darlin'," Ciel drawled.

"He's a fine-looking man," Lauren offered as she watched Whiskey Bay's main-street traffic through the wide plate-glass windows. In front of the *Press* office, a man in a tank top and a New Orleans Saints cap poured root beer into barrels of red geraniums wilting in the noonday sun.

"We march to different drummers. Kinda like Charlie Reynolds there." Ciel kept her tone light to prove she wasn't nursing a broken heart.

Izzy was a decent guy, but so *predictable*. It made Ciel feel petty to want more—excitement, adventure, *something!*—out of a relationship, but there it was. Eligible men were few and far between in Whiskey Bay for women of her "advanced" years, but Izzy just didn't light any fires. And she refused to settle for a man by default or out of some mistaken romantic notion she was certain to regret. It wasn't fair to Izzy, who deserved better, and it wasn't fair to her.

Ciel let her thoughts drift briefly to the startling encounter she'd had five days earlier—to a pair of tawny eyes, jet-black hair, a physique that did as much for a pair of faded jeans and T-shirt as Antonio Banderas did, and a full mouth sculpted for pure pleasure despite its unfortunate tendency to remain straight and unsmiling. Too bad he was such a stiff old stick, and a hermit, to boot! Scowling, Ciel put the annoying and enigmatic Jack Cooper firmly out of her mind.

"My, my, my," Lauren murmured, her dark eyes narrowing with interest as a van painted an institutional tan parked on the street and the driver climbed out. "Don't look now, darlin', but I've just found the man I'd leave Tiny for."

Ciel's fingers slipped, and she yelped as she peeled the skin off a knuckle. "What!"

"Just teasing, honey." Lauren laughed, her red-tinted lips pursed in a seductive pout. "But, *yum,* if you know what I mean."

"Close your mouth," Ciel advised tartly. "You're drooling on your chest. I'd hate for you to electrocute yourself when you touch the keyboard."

"Wouldn't be the only sparks flying today," Lauren commented wickedly. "I wonder who he is—oh, my God! He's coming in here!"

Sucking her sore knuckle, Ciel glanced up, then promptly forgot what she was doing, as Jack Cooper walked into the office.

Even in her distracted state the other night, she'd known the man was good-looking, but in the bright light of day, the whole package was awe inspiring. Tall, broad-shouldered, he had chest muscles that rippled impressively under that same spaceship T-shirt he'd almost made into a tourniquet. Soft denim outlined his lean flanks and new, expensive running shoes gave mute testimony to an athleticism that surely accounted for his lanky, pantherlike grace.

Disappointingly, his remarkable golden brown eyes were hidden behind a pair of Ray·Ban sunglasses. Radiating pure masculinity, his very presence left Ciel annoyingly breathless.

"May I help you with something, sir?" Lauren practically purred the question. Though she adored her husband, when confronted with a male specimen this magnificent all Lauren's feminine instincts kicked in. If she'd been a pinball machine, every light and whistle would have been going off.

He retrieved a slip of paper from his front jeans pocket, stretching the worn fabric in a most intimate and breath-stealing manner. "I'd like to place this posted notice in your paper."

At the sound of Jack's deep Western drawl, Ciel gave a start, and realized she was trying to swallow her knuckle. Hastily removing it from her mouth, she stuck her hand in the pocket of her beige pants. With his strong nose and square chin, Jack Cooper was certainly moviestar handsome, but his tone was coolly unemotional, sexy and chilling and mysterious all at the same time. Despite the temperature rising both outside and inside the overheated office, she shivered, then stifled an inward groan.

Good Lord! She must be sunstruck, because she certainly wasn't that man starved! She'd had an almost fiancé in college, and while her social life hadn't been exactly scintillating by big-city standards since then, she was not—repeat *not*—a quivering twenty-eight-year-old virgin ready to be bowled over by the first presentable male to darken Whiskey Bay's doorstep in years.

To prove it to herself, she hastily dipped her head and reapplied herself to fitting the computer circuit board back into place. To her immense frustration, it still wouldn't fit.

"We'll get it in this week's edition," Lauren was saying. She smiled at Jack as if he'd just ensured the continued existence of the free world. "Anything else?"

"And some of those No Trespassing signs, too."

He pointed in the direction of a revolving display rack. "Better make it a full dozen."

The request made Ciel's hackles rise. How typically male! Despite her advice, he still intended to fling neighborly courtesy to the winds! Just who the hell did he think he was?

Unable to contain her irritation, Ciel strode toward the front counter, a circuit board in one hand. "Hi, Jack! Still expecting visitors? Pity you haven't read my last editorial on Southern hospitality."

Lifting his head, Jack Cooper peered at her through those dark, blank lenses for a long, unnerving moment.

"A reporter," he muttered finally. "I might have known."

Ciel bristled. "You were expecting maybe Anne Rice in an eyeshade?"

Lauren, who had observed this exchange with interest, lifted an inquisitive eyebrow, so Ciel took the hint and made introductions. "This is my office manager, Lauren Herbert. Lauren, Jack Cooper. The boys and I...er, ran into him a few days ago. He's staying at the old Ballard place."

Lauren smiled widely at Jack. "Pleased to meet you. What brings you to our little town, Mr. Cooper?"

"Peace and quiet," Jack said.

Ciel could have sworn the temperature in the office dropped twenty degrees. It was amazing what the man could do for climate control with a mere look. If he could harness that talent as a new technology, he'd make a fortune, not to mention save on his utility bills.

"Well, you're certain to get plenty of quiet around here!" Lauren said with a breathy laugh. "Nothing ever happens in Whiskey Bay."

"I live in hope." Jack reached into his back pocket for his wallet and began to pull out bills. "How much do I owe you?"

Ciel broke in before Lauren could reply. "Twenty for the notice, a buck apiece for the signs, tax—say thirty-five even." She ignored the startled look Lauren gave her.

Wordlessly, he counted out bills and pushed them across the counter, then picked up his signs.

Ciel's fingertips tapped out an irritated rhythm on the computer board. "Anyone with half a brain can see it's going to be more trouble keeping folks away than simply letting things be, but I don't suppose you believe that."

His mouth tightened. "No."

Ciel gave an "it's-no-skin-off-my-nose" shrug. "Suit yourself."

"I intend to. And by the way, anyone with half a brain would know that a circuit board will work better if it's installed right side up."

Incensed, Ciel thrust the circuit board at Jack. "Well...well, if you're so smart, be my guest!"

A muscle in Jack's jaw twitched, but to Ciel's immense surprise, he took the board and walked around the counter to the table littered with machine parts. Pulling off his sunglasses, he hooked the stem into the crew neck of his knit shirt, flipped the board over, then slipped it into the appropriate slot inside the typesetter. It snapped right into place.

Ciel looked at Lauren. "I *knew* that." Jack flipped a switch, and the computer beeped and hummed into life. "I knew *that,* too!"

Lauren propped her chin on her fist and gave her friend a sultry, amused look. "Say, who was that masked man, Tonto?"

As if in answer, the typesetter beeped and immediately went dead again.

Ciel swore. "Hellfire and damnation!"

"I wouldn't recommend it," Jack said quietly.

"Recommend what?"

Jack's voice was solemn, but the faint tilt of one dark eyebrow betrayed his amusement. "Bad-mouthing the machinery. Invariably, it'll hear and understand. And make you pay."

Surprised, Ciel couldn't contain a laugh. "Not superstitious, are you?"

"Hey." He shrugged broad shoulders. "I don't argue with facts. And I don't cuss sensitive electronic machines. Makes 'em cantankerous."

"I'll swear off swearing permanently if it'll make a difference," she said, sighing. "I can't do anything with this stupid machine!"

Jack hit the switch, then pulled the board free again and picked at the printed circuits with a fingernail. "Well, here's part of the trouble…hmm, let me have a look at this other panel.…"

"Would you?" Ciel mentally took back every nasty thought she'd ever had about Jack Cooper. "That would be very kind of you."

"No problem." He was already engrossed in the mysteries of the electronic monster.

"Well, I think I'll go on over to the bank to set the rest of that type," Lauren announced, gathering up a folder of copy. "Nice to meet you, Mr. Cooper."

Lost in the innards of the computer, Jack murmured something polite and gave a distracted wave. Ciel followed Lauren as far as the door, bending her head when her petite friend crooked her finger.

"Why'd you charge him double for everything,

Ciel?'' Lauren whispered, dimpling mischievously. ''All that animal magnetism rubbing you the wrong way?''

A small pleat formed between Ciel's arched brows. ''Don't be ridiculous. The man may be a computer whiz, but he's got the personality and manners of a donkey.''

''That isn't exactly the way I'd describe him,'' Lauren drawled, then let out a lusty sigh. ''Hunky. Gorgeous. Built. Too bad my Tiny's the jealous type—just kidding, Ciel!''

Brushing curls out of her eyes, Ciel chuckled and gave Lauren a push toward the entrance. ''You'd better be!''

''I wouldn't trade Tiny for anything, but if you don't see what I'm talking about and make a move on this guy pronto, *you're* the one who'd better have her head examined!''

With a wink, Lauren sailed through the front door, and Ciel went back to watch Jack Cooper. He might be an annoying individual, but beggars couldn't be choosers when it came to free computer service!

''Think there's any hope for it?'' she asked at his elbow.

''Too soon to really tell.''

Ciel jammed her fingers through her red-gold waves, then reclipped the mass of hair at her nape with a wide metal barrette and sighed in resignation.

''I guess Lauren can set the rest of the front page at the bank. Not that we're going to have that much news this week anyway. The mayor canceled the town council meeting due to lack of interest, so the only big story I have is the mental patient who stole Mrs. Lausin's Bimmer from in front of the Circle K.''

''Let me guess. That's him at the front window now.''

Ciel looked up to find Charlie Reynolds engrossed in a finger game of Eensy-Weensy Spider. She wagged her fingers at him. He laughed soundlessly on the other side of the glass, waved back and ambled off in search of another diversion.

"That's just Charlie," she told Jack. "He's harmless. My geraniums have never looked so good since he's been doping them with the cases of root beer he won at the VFW dance contest."

"Some of that local Southern color I've heard so much about? Or has he just been out in the sun too long?"

"Maybe some of both," she admitted wryly. "Anyway, the state police picked up that hospital patient joyriding in Lafayette half an hour ago."

Jack quit poking at the electronic pathways inside the machine long enough to give Ciel a curious look. "How did you find that out so fast?"

"Well, I've got a scanner in my car, but actually, my mother called to tell me." Ciel propped her elbows on the desk and gave Jack a wry grin. "She's a more reliable source anyway."

"You don't say." His expression quizzical, Jack began to reassemble the typesetter.

Ciel nodded. "Mama knows everything, or can find it out. Comes in handy around here. Of course, growing up, my brothers and sisters really hated that her radar was so good. Couldn't get away with a damn thing."

"Big family?"

"I've got five brothers and sisters," Ciel replied. The easy chitchat between her and Stoneface Cooper surprised her, but she wasn't about to call attention to the fact that they actually seemed to be having a conversation. "My dad passed away a while back. You?"

"Just my father and me, as long as I can remember.

He's retired from the air force now. Lives in Tulsa. I don't see much of him.''

"That's too bad." Ciel watched Jack competently check the old computer, admiring the efficiency of his movements and the lack of wasted motion that indicated extensive training. "I can't imagine not having a lot of family around all the time. So, how's your pond scum coming along?''

Jack glanced up sharply, then his features relaxed when he saw she was teasing him. "Pretty disgusting."

"That well, huh?''

"Not too bad." The corners of his mouth lifted slightly, then he was all seriousness again.

But Ciel had seen it. A real smile. A first from Jack Cooper. It pleased her immensely and made something odd tickle in the back of her throat. He didn't seem the kind of man who smiled easily, which was a pity, because when he did, that handsome face of his was truly devastating. And he'd smiled at *her*.

But that was dangerous and uncharted territory. Out of self-defense, Ciel dropped her gaze to his chest, but that expanse of muscle, barely hidden under the stretched-tight old shirt, with the little dark curls of chest hair peeking out at the neck, was just as perilous for a girl's equilibrium as his face. Bemused by this realization, Ciel frowned at the logo on his shirt, then snapped her fingers.

"That reminds me.''

"Hmm?" He was engrossed, intent on his task.

"Oh, nothing. I just promised Kyle I'd try to find something for him.''

Ciel sauntered over to an old metal file cabinet where she stored all the press releases, giveaways and promotional mailings the *Press* received. Kyle and Tony had been talking about rockets, Obiwan Kenobi and the starship *Enterprise* all week, and if she wasn't mistaken, she'd saved some old black-and-white photos from NASA that they could pin up like posters in their rooms.

She riffled through the first drawer and removed a fat file. Plopping down in Lauren's steno chair with the file in her lap, she began to sort through the mess of papers.

"Here's your problem." Jack held up a board. "But the whole thing's so obsolete you'd be better off junking it, Ciel."

She looked up with a sigh. "That's what I was afraid of. Unfortunately the *Press*'s budget doesn't run to new equipment right now."

Jack considered for a moment. "If I solder a few of these loose points, it might work awhile longer. Worth a try."

"There's the solder gun. Have at it," she said. "If you're sure this won't take too much of your time."

His reply was dry, but he was already reaching for the soldering iron. "Things have been relatively quiet at the camp. I can spare a minute."

"The boys won't go near for fear of their lives."

"Well, perhaps I was a trifle hasty...there." He held up the board to inspect his work, waved it to cool the solder, then inserted it into the machine.

Idly sifting through the file, Ciel gently pressed the boys' case. "I'm sure they'd be very careful not to disturb you, Jack, and in return for fishing privileges they could save you some time and hang those signs for you—*oh, my God.*"

Jack flipped the switch on the typesetter, which hummed quietly, then flashed into life. "Good as new," he said with satisfaction, then caught sight of Ciel's astonished expression. "Now what's wrong?"

Ciel held up a glossy eight-by-ten photo. A group of men and women in blue jumpsuits stood in front of a giant rendering of the same logo that adorned his shirt.

"Dr. J. C. Cooper! Why didn't you tell me you were an *astronaut?*"

Something like alarm flickered across Jack's features. "Look, Ciel—"

"Don't tell me this isn't you," she interrupted, jumping to her feet and tapping his image with her fingertip.

"No, that's me." Jack admitted, rubbing the back of his neck as if he'd just discovered a royal pain there. "And the title is 'mission specialist.' But I'm basically a biologist."

"'Ph.D exobiologist...bachelor...three shuttle trips,'" she read from the cutline, then looked up at him in pure amazement. "Why wouldn't you mention such a thing? I'd be so proud—did they kick you out or something?"

"Of course not!" Jack's shocked expression was almost comical. Exasperated, he shoved his fingers through his hair. "I retired from NASA to pursue private work. I'm trying to develop algae that will grow the oxygen supply on a space station."

"Well—well, that's *wonderful!*" Ciel beamed like a little girl who'd opened the best Christmas present in the world. "Wait until everyone hears this. Imagine you being right here in Whiskey Bay doing such important work. I'll do an interview—"

"Hold everything, damn it!" Jack seemed to realize how harsh that sounded and, with a visible effort, moderated his tone. "Look, Ciel, my work is the very reason I'm here. If I don't get my grant proposal in under deadline, I can kiss it all goodbye."

Bewildered, she stared at him. "But, Jack—"

"Do you honestly think I would have the solitude I need if you print a story in the *Press?* I'll have autograph hounds and curiosity seekers coming out the kazoo, and no amount of No Trespassing signs will stop them. I'd have to go back to Houston, and God knows I wasn't accomplishing anything there! The time I took moving everything here would be for nothing."

"You mean, if I tell anyone who you really are, you're afraid your whole project will fold?" she asked in a small voice.

"I can almost predict it." He heaved a deep breath, feeling both desperate and resigned. "Look, Ciel, I don't want to seem mean spirited, but I'm under tremendous pressure. This project—well, it means everything to me. It's only for a few weeks. Keep this under your hat, and when I'm done, I'll be glad to give you an interview."

"Uh. That's reasonable, I guess."

"Then I can depend on your discretion?"

Thoughtfully, she stroked her chin with her forefinger. "I've never met anyone who's actually been in space. It's all so...fascinating."

A muscle in Jack's jaw jumped angrily. "Yeah, well, I never met a reporter who could keep a confidence."

"Then it's clear you've been hanging out with the wrong crowd, Dr. Cooper."

"Isn't there anything I can do to convince you?" he asked wearily.

Ciel replaced the photo in her folder and studied Jack Cooper. Without a doubt, he was the most intriguing man to cross her path in quite a long time. He was also one of the most aggravating. Why, he'd practically insulted her integrity, and just when she'd been on the point of deciding he wasn't nearly as obnoxious an individual as she had thought! Still, since he wasn't the only one with a secret project, it might be interesting to get to know him a little better. All in all, the opportunity was too perfect to resist.

"Don't look so worried, Dr. Cooper," she advised him sweetly. "I owe you, after all, for fixing my typesetter. All I want from you is some information and…"

"And what?" he asked suspiciously.

Ciel smiled. "Lunch."

IT WAS REMARKABLE how a bowl of the best seafood gumbo he had ever tasted could alter a man's outlook, Jack decided.

He lounged in his chair like a sleepy, well-fed lion, watching Ciel sip the last of her iced tea. They were the only ones left from the lunch crowd at Benoît's Lakeside Café. Ceiling fans whirred softly over their heads on the tiny screened-in dining porch facing the glistening water. She pushed the plate with the last piece of crusty French bread toward him, but he shook his head.

"Let me get this straight," he said. "You say you write science fiction?"

"On the side." Nervously, Ciel pleated her paper napkin between her fingertips, her expression suddenly, but charmingly, shy. "But you probably hear this kind of thing all the time."

"Not as often as you'd suppose," Jack drawled.

A stomach full of the first truly tasty food in nearly a week made Jack feel mellow through and through. And the fact that a female reporter sat opposite him—an attractive, vivacious female reporter whose skin was like cream and whose smile could melt moon rock at a thousand parsecs—didn't alarm him as much as he knew it should.

"I'm simply a little surprised that you're interested in that kind of thing," he continued.

"I've been a fan since I was young. While my friends were reading Nancy Drew, I was gobbling up Isaac Asimov, Robert Heinlein and Ursula Le Guim. So when Sylvie—that's my heroine's name, Sylvie Fairstar—popped into my head one day, it seemed natural to write down her story." Ciel lifted her shoulders, and her mouth twisted into a rueful moue. "That manuscript has been sent to so many publishers I've little hope of it ever selling, but I've got it out there again, so who knows?"

"And now you're writing a second book about this Sylvie?"

"I'm about halfway through," Ciel said, nodding. "Maybe someday there will be a series featuring Sylvie's psi-clone adventures. Anyway, it's fun. But my imagination tends go off on tangents about actual scientific possibilities. If you could help me unravel some of the technical knots I've written myself into..."

"Then you'll keep mum about my illustrious past," Jack finished dryly.

Ciel grinned, unrepentant. "Do we have a deal?"

"How can I refuse?" he said. "You've got me over a barrel."

"It's a trade-off. Actually..."

While her fingers mangled the paper napkin into tatters, her teeth bit at her lush lower lip. The unconsciously provocative action caught Jack's gaze, and his mouth went dry. He had to forcibly drag his attention back to what she had been saying.

"Actually, what?"

"Actually, no one knows that I'm writing a book," she said in a rush. "I've never told anyone until now."

Her admission produced a strange jolt that hit Jack low in the gut. "Not even your family?"

She shook her head. "Some dreams aren't for sharing. I've been almost afraid to say anything, like it would hex me or something." She laughed. "That sounds as loony as Mrs. Jessup and her flashlight burglars. The heat must be getting to me, too!"

Admiring her self-deprecating humor, Jack felt a little humbled and touched that she'd shared her secret with him. Hell, he had dreams of his own. It wouldn't kill him to cooperate. "What kind of things do you want to know?"

"Oh, everything." Her expression was suddenly wistful. "When I think of all the adventures you've had—"

Jack's mouth tightened. "Don't glamorize it, Ciel. It was damned hard and dangerous work. Still is."

She looked down, seemed surprised at the shredded napkin, then tossed it aside. "I suppose you have to think of it that way to function well. But tell me, what does it feel like? Is it as marvelous to float above the Earth as I think it is?"

"You're normally too busy to marvel much."

"You cynic," she jeered softly. "You must have a heart of stone to remain unmoved by such an achievement! Weren't you the least bit awed?"

He sobered. "Yeah. Yeah, I was."

"I knew you were faking, Astronaut Cooper."

"Call me that again and I'm liable to wring your pretty neck," he warned lazily.

Blushing, she unclipped her hair and lifted the mass of curls off the neck in question, then gave him a smile. "All right, Jack. I'll try not to antagonize my scientific expert any more than necessary. At least until you tell me all you know about silicon-based life forms."

Barely curbing the urge to reach over and bury his hands in her hair, Jack began to talk. Ciel listened raptly and plied him with intelligent questions while François brought coffee and, on Ciel's orders, the house specialty of bread pudding with rum sauce.

But when François came back to their table offering second cups of the black-as-sin south Louisiana brew, Ciel glanced at her watch and stifled a gasp of dismay.

"Oh, Lord! I've got to get back. Jack, I'm sorry. I didn't mean to tie you up all afternoon—"

He was already on his feet, pulling back her chair for her, reaching for his wallet and ignoring a sense of disappointment that this unexpectedly pleasant interlude should be ending so soon. "I needed the break and the food, I'm sure. I'll just get this…"

"No, put your money back," Ciel ordered, grabbing her shoulder bag from the back of the chair. "I already took care of the tab." She fixed him with an impish look when he opened his mouth to protest. "No arguments, Professor!"

Jack had no recourse but to follow her out of the rustic restaurant and across the blistering parking lot, where they'd parked his beat-up van and her ancient green Camaro. Ciel tossed her bag in through her car's open window and paused beside the driver's door.

"Are you always so adroit at maneuvering people to get your way?" Jack complained.

Squinting against the sun's brightness, she dimpled and leaned her hip gingerly against the car's fender. "Mostly."

"I can imagine," Jack said with a chuckle.

Then he gave in to the impulse he'd been trying to resist and tangled his fingers in a lock of her hair. Silky, springy, it curled like a cool flame over his skin. Ciel stood very still, her eyes wide and cautious, while behind her the radio scanner inside her car crackled, alternating static with brief, nearly indecipherable words.

He could see the pulse leap at the base of her throat as he touched her fiery hair, and an answering beat throbbed in his groin. She was luscious. Lovely in a totally unselfconscious way. Not another woman of his acquaintance could have resisted camouflaging those adorable freckles under a layer of makeup or ruthlessly subduing those springy curls into some kind of lacquered helmet. It made him wonder if that kind of freedom carried over into other areas of her life—like in bed. The thought made him reckless.

"To look at you," Jack mused, "no one would ever guess you're not above a little polite blackmail, either."

"That's a bit harsh, isn't it?" she murmured. "After all, I did buy you lunch."

Jack gave a bark of laughter and slid his hand down her shoulder to where the tender curve of her elbow was revealed by the cuff of her white sleeve. "And so you ought, considering how you gouged me for the cost of the ad and those signs!"

Ciel blinked, then a hot tide of color flooded her face. "Oh, darn," she said weakly.

He made circles in the sensitive crook of her elbow with his thumb, smiling wickedly as he felt the prickle of gooseflesh pebble her skin. "Call it even?"

She tilted her chin upward to meet his subtle challenge, presenting Jack an enticing view of her perfect, peachy mouth.

"Only if you're willing to answer more questions about extraterrestrial exploration and light speeds."

"Maybe I'll submit to a second round of blackmail, but what if I don't?" he growled.

"Then I'd be forced to blab everything I know about the famous astronaut in our midst," she threatened airily.

Placing his free hand on the car roof behind her, he made a cage with his body and the car. His gaze dropped to her upturned mouth. "There are ways to silence you, woman."

An intangible tension flared and crackled between them like lightning. The atmosphere seemed suddenly dangerously charged. From a great distance, a rumble of thunder threatened.

"In fact," Jack continued, hardly recognizing the hungry, husky note in his voice, "I'd lay odds that mouth of yours is going to get you into big trouble someday."

"A girl can hope, can't she?" Ciel returned, her tone jaunty but her smile wobbling dangerously.

"Big, big trouble," he muttered.

And for no earthly reason he could think of, it was suddenly imperative that Jack taste that tempting mouth. But the instant he bent his head, the scanner inside the car gave a squawk. Ciel jumped, ducked under Jack's arm and tilted an ear toward the flurry of conversation pouring over the radio.

"Lord-a-mercy, something's going on!" She reached for the door handle. "Could mean a picture for the front page. I'd better go."

"Um, sure." Jack stepped back as she scrambled into the vehicle. He didn't know whether he was more frustrated or relieved.

Ciel cranked the ignition, then flashed him a bright, apologetic smile. "Well. See you, Jack."

He gave her a brief salute, then watched her spin out

of the parking lot, spewing gravel as if the devil himself were on her tail.

Ciel's sudden fit of skittishness surprised him. What the hell, he thought. Ciel Landry was a problem he didn't need. He certainly didn't have time or energy for complications, flirtations, literary consultations or anything else but pond scum for the duration! Hands shoved inside his back pockets, Jack watched her car disappear down the dusty road.

CIEL WAS unpleasantly surprised to discover how difficult it was to drive when one's knees had been reduced to the consistency of gelatin by the laser-beam gaze of a sexy biologist and the sheer certainty that if not for the hand of Providence she would at this moment be experiencing meltdown in the arms of one Jack Cooper! Trying to control her shaking limbs, she automatically tuned the scanner, then turned the vehicle toward the location of the call. Whatever her personal turmoil, there was a newspaper to get out tomorrow, and she needed a lead photo.

But she was confused, bemused and befuddled, to say the least. Why would a man who'd repeatedly insisted he wanted to be left alone stoop to kissing a lowly small-town reporter? Curiosity? Boredom? As a warning that she was pushing him too far?

Only, he hadn't kissed her, of course.

Rats! No, she thought, *thank goodness! No, oh...oh, phooey!*

Despite Lauren's advice, Ciel had better things to do than set herself up for a fall with a man who was only going to be in Whiskey Bay temporarily, even if he was gorgeous and sexy as hell.

And extremely intelligent. And obviously ambitious. And had masculine charisma oozing from every pore.

Ciel tried not to let her very vivid imagination draw mental pictures of what it would be like to be kissed by Jack Cooper—the pressure of his lips against hers, his warmth, his unique taste. Heat rose in her body, melting her in places she didn't want to think about. Ciel hit the switches on her air conditioner, remembered she hadn't gotten it fixed yet, and mouthed a succinct expletive that would have once caused Marie to wash her mouth out with soap.

Fuming, Ciel scarcely realized that the police call was taking her down the road past the Ballard camp. She followed the rutted gravel track a half mile farther, threading through cultivated rice land of curved terraces and levees. This late in the season the paddies were dry and the rice plants heavy headed with their ripening harvest. She pulled up behind several deputy sheriffs' tan-and-white cars parked on the edge of the road, just as the air rumbled with a clap of thunder.

Come on and rain! Ciel prayed. Anything to cool off the summer lunatics in Whiskey Bay! Including one Ciel Landry.

Squinting against the police cars' flashing blue lights, Ciel grabbed her camera from the back seat and scrambled out. A clump of officers in khaki uniforms and gun belts stood on top of the nearest levee with a couple of jeans-clad farmers. Farther down, another deputy threaded his way through the field of waving grain toward a distant patch. Putting Jack Cooper out of her mind, Ciel hurried up behind a stocky black officer she recognized.

"What's going on, Cleveland?"

"Hey, Ciel." Deputy Sheriff Cleveland Henderson

held his billed service cap in one hand and scratched his graying pate with the other. "Damned if I know. Never saw anything like it."

Puzzled, Ciel frowned, straining to see what had captured their attention. "What—oh, my gosh! Would you look at that!"

In the center of the field a perfectly circular section fifty yards in diameter had been absolutely flattened, the rice plants crushed and blackened. A scorched path that looked like some sort of exhaust trail ran from the main circle toward the road before disappearing.

"What in the world is that?" Ciel wondered, already lifting her camera and firing off shots. There was something vaguely familiar in the pattern. Where had she seen this before?

"You got me," Cleveland said. "Just appeared overnight, and nobody's seen anything like it. Not the county agent or the fellow who leases these acres from the parish or even Doc Anderson. Everybody's stumped."

"What about you, Cleveland?" Ciel squatted to get a better angle on the officers examining the mutilated rice. "Any ideas, on or off the record?"

"Mighty strange things been going on around here lately," he muttered. "This dang heat..."

"Don't I know it!" she agreed fervently. A single huge raindrop splashed in the dry dirt at her feet. Then another. The earthy smell of dust and moisture rose to her nostrils.

"Sheriff Lesieur said...well, never you mind that."

"What?" When the deputy didn't answer, Ciel looked up from adjusting her lens cover to protect the camera from the slowly approaching shower. "Cleveland?"

He jammed his cap on his head and folded his arms

across his chest in a belligerent stance. "Don't quote me now, Ciel."

"Just spill it, will you?" she said with an exasperated laugh.

Cleveland turned his dark-brown eyes on her. "Don't it look like something just squatted down out there? Something big?"

Ciel stared, uncomprehending, then gasped as the scene in front of her clicked in with the memory of something she'd only read about. She jumped to her feet. "Surely you don't mean—"

"Yes'm." The deputy nodded solemnly. "If I didn't know better, I'd say we've had us a visit—from a gol-darned flying saucer!"

3

UFO's Land In Whiskey Bay?

The headline blared the news in six-inch type. Easy to read, especially when someone was practically shoving newsprint up your nose.

"Are you out of your ever-lovin' mind?"

"I wasn't the last time I looked in the mirror, *Mr. Mayor*." Stopping just inside the *Press*'s front office door, Ciel hooked her dripping umbrella over the front page Emile Nabors was brandishing in her face and pushed it aside.

After pulling an all-nighter to get the paper out, the last thing Ciel wanted in her rushed, sleepy and caffeine-deprived state was to find a red-faced, irate politician on her doorstep. Tossing down the umbrella, she shook the moisture from her out-of-control curls and limp black skirt. The much-welcome drizzle had fizzled out on her drive into work, and the sun was turning the town into a steambath.

"I know you're responsible for this...this lunacy!" Glaring at her, Emile rattled the latest edition of the *Press* in her face again. He was in his midfifties, and his sandy hair was just beginning to show gray; his ruddy complexion displayed his love of the bottle and his disposition.

Ciel took the paper, perused the photo of the flattened rice field and the accompanying headline carefully, then swung her gaze to Lauren, who stood behind the counter, nervously popping her gum. "Actually, that headline was supposed to read Summer Madness."

Lauren pursed her carmine-tinted lips and casually adjusted the straps of her crimson tank top. "The typesetter went on the fritz right after you left last night, so I improvised and used the alphabet off a printing-supply calendar."

"Why didn't you set the original lead?" Ciel asked.

Lauren shrugged, grinning. "Weren't enough *M*s."

"Well, this is much better. Good work."

"What!" Emile squawked. "I've never heard of anything so totally irresponsible! Couldn't believe my eyes when I picked up doughnuts at the E-Z Eats and saw this in the rack. Are you trying to start a panic?"

"You mean like when Orson Welles broadcast 'War of the Worlds' over the radio, and half the American public really thought the Martians were attacking and the world as they knew it was coming to an end?" Ciel's eyes sparkled. "That'd be great, wouldn't it?"

"It's a disaster—that's what it is! We'll be the laughingstock of the entire state! UFOs! I tell you this is an outrage! I demand that you retrieve every single issue."

"Can't," Lauren said smugly. "Took them to the post office an hour ago."

"What?" Emile's color darkened to a stroke-inducing crimson.

Out of patience with the mayor's theatrics, Ciel nevertheless kept her tone sugar sweet and placating. "As a public servant yourself, Emile, you understand that we can't buck the U.S. government."

"But flying saucers in Whiskey Bay! How could you print such a whopper? That's not journalism and you know it, but I guess it's no more than we can expect from you.''

Ciel scowled. "Just what is that supposed to mean? And have you even bothered to read my lead article? No, I see you haven't. Listen up.''

She read aloud:

Whiskey Bay added another chronicle to its list of unusual events chalked up to the August dog days this week. Leaseholder Calvin Dugin lost nearly half an acre of rice this past Monday night when a mysterious blight flattened his crop just off Ballard Road. Destroyed was a geometrically perfect fifty-foot circle of grain.

"Ain't rot. Ain't critters. Ain't natural. Never seen anything like it," Dugin said.

Parish agricultural agent Les Loftin could offer no explanation, either, except to point out that similar phenomena occurred in English cornfields some years back. Interested observers attributed the curiosity to visitors from space, but others called it a hoax.

"There's a logical, scientific explanation," Loftin says, but when pressed admits that he has none at this point. While one unnamed source suggested flying saucers might be responsible, and local cases of summer madness are at an all-time high, readers must draw their own conclusions. Local authorities are continuing the investigation. In other news...

Ciel looked up at Emile. "There. What's inflammatory about that?''

"You practically said we'd been invaded, that's what!" Emile snapped.

Lauren hugged herself and shivered deliciously. "It's so exciting. 'We are not alone.' Imagine that!"

"That's exactly the kind of thing we *don't* need," Emile howled. He pointed a stubby finger at Ciel's nose. "If this thing gets out of hand, I'm going to call a town council meeting and hold you personally responsible, Ciel Landry!"

"You're the one getting out of hand, Emile. Why, the rest of the article is very tongue-in-cheek about all the weird things happening around here lately."

She ran a finger down the column of print, quoting the sidebar headlines. "Streaker Lincoln Dobbs Arrested For Indecent Exposure. Adelaide Posner Sets Speed Record In Classic Car. Nap Conly Imitates Submarine. It's supposed to be humorous, for goodness sakes!"

"I don't see anything remotely funny about holding our town and its citizens up to ridicule!"

"You wouldn't," Lauren muttered.

Emile whirled on her, still pointing. "Just as I thought! I just hope I can salvage the town's image somehow."

"You're overreacting, Mayor. Making a mountain out of a molehill."

"Oh, really?" Emile's eyes narrowed. "Then explain why there's already such a traffic jam on Ballard Road the sheriff called in an extra deputy to direct cars."

"You're kidding." Delight brightened her smile. "That's wonderful! Have you seen the landing site? It really looks great. No Eighth Wonder of the World, of course, but—"

"Would you be serious? The curiosity seekers are clogging up the main arteries trying to get to it. Why, Sonny Prejean called to complain that his dump trucks can't even get to the landfill. Prejean Oil and Engineering is a big taxpayer in this county. The last thing we need is to give our local businessmen trouble!''

"I'm sure Somy will survive."

"You just get ready to print a retraction in next week's paper."

Ciel stiffened. To have this buffoon question her journalistic integrity made her grind her teeth. "I stand by my work, Emile."

"It's on your head, then, and God help us all!"

Turning on his heel, the mayor stormed out of the office, much to Ciel's relief.

"I'm sorry about all that," Lauren said. "I guess I shouldn't have changed that headline."

"Don't worry about it." Rounding the counter toward her desk, Ciel gave her a half-rueful, half-mischievous smile. "It was worth it to get under Emile's skin— again."

Lauren's eyes sparkled. "Yeah, you're kinda like his own personal brand of itching powder, aren't you?"

"If he spent as much time on town business as he does on trying to look like a mover and shaker, Whiskey Bay would be a lot better off."

"Maybe someone will run against him next time."

"Or maybe our visiting aliens will kidnap him." Ciel laughed. "I can see the headlines now. Mayor Abducted By Aliens. Town Celebrates."

Lauren shuddered. "That landing site stuff is kind of spooky. Do you think we really had a close encounter?"

"I hope so. We could stand some stirring up around here." Ciel grinned and hummed a snatch of "The X Files" theme song. "What do you think? Ready for a visit from agents Mulder and Scully?"

"Yes!"

The phone rang, and Lauren sauntered to the receiver, laughing. "You're nuts."

The front door rattled. A corpulent couple in Tweedledee and Tweedledum striped shirts waddled in.

"Howdy, there, honey!" Dum boomed. A Nikon swung from his neck.

"Can you direct us to the launch pad?" Dee asked from behind a pair of sunflower-yellow sunglasses.

Ciel blinked. "Ah—"

"Hey, Ciel!" Lauren hollered, scribbling on a notepad as the phone pealed again.

"Mitzy's got a hankering to see that there rocket ship," Dum explained.

"Had a cousin was snatched back in '57," Dee confided. "Nobody believed her but me."

"You don't say." Ciel blinked again. "Well, you're looking for Ballard Road—"

Lauren bounced to Ciel's side, shoving phone messages into her hand. "That was Izzy. He says bring your camera over to the Stop and Go. Lance Fontenot's Chrysler keeps turning itself off and on with no key and no driver."

Ciel shuffled through the notes, mystified. "What's happening around here?"

"Isn't that what a hotshot reporter is supposed to check out?" Lauren shot back, grinning.

"Right! Okay, I'm on my way."

"Oops, there's that phone again!" Lauren went to grab it.

"Could you hurry it up, honey?" Dum asked cheerfully. "Want to beat the crowds. Tourists, you know. Not professionals like me and Mitzy."

"Of course. A crush can be so inconvenient—" A

thought struck Ciel, and she groaned. "Lord, that road leads right past Uncle Etienne's camp!"

"So?" Dee asked expectantly.

"So?" Dum echoed curiously.

"So?" Lauren said, poised with one red-enameled fingertip over the pealing phone.

Ciel rolled her eyes and groaned again. "So Dr. Recluse himself, Jack Cooper, is sitting smack-dab in the middle of a stream of unwelcome visitors—and he's going to blame me!"

"FIREFLIES. All flickery, you know? And noisy, too. Tapping and knocking like woodpeckers."

"Now, Miss Sally," Ciel asked, "are you positive?"

Bent, but still spry under her bib apron, Sally Jessup nodded her tight blue-rinse curls and pointed to the eaves of her frame house. "Right up there, sis. Dadgum burglars, every night. Last time I'll vote for Sheriff Lesieur. Law enforcement—ha!"

"But nothing's been stolen, you say?" Ciel scribbled madly in her steno notebook.

"A lady's got to learn to take care of herself, sis." With a sly grin, Miss Sally lifted her apron and patted the .357 Magnum stuck in her waistband.

"MR. DOBBS, er, could you—if you don't mind!" Ciel flushed and fanned herself with her notebook.

"Sorry." Lincoln Dobbs repositioned the plastic trash-can lid over his lower body and stretched out on the concrete picnic table. Ciel noted that he was getting quite a good all-over tan for a paunchy middle-aged insurance salesman.

"And you say your new interest in nudism isn't an attempt to get back in touch with nature?" She looked up to find a couple of uniformed officers hurrying across the public park toward them.

"What an insane notion." He set two little eye cups in place, stretched out in the sun and gave a sigh of contentment. "I'm absorbing gamma radiation from Alpha Centauri."

"YEAH?" JACK GLARED at the young man in the "Keep Trekking" T-shirt banging on his door.

"Looking for that 'ere flying saucer. This the place?" A folded copy of the *Whiskey Bay Press* with its blazing UFO headline stuck out of the intruder's back pocket. The barefoot toddler perched on his hip grinned toothily at Jack.

The question had been repeated so often Jack didn't even answer, just pointed down the road.

"Tommy's got to go. Do you mind?"

Jack started to point out the hand-lettered sign he'd posted on the front railing that said No Public Facilities, but that sign was having just about as much effect as the No Trespassing notices posted on every conceivable tree and fence post in the immediate vicinity of the camp house—which meant exactly zero. And the toddler's strained expression and beseeching blue eyes undid Jack's resolve.

"In there," he growled, jerking his thumb. "But don't either of you touch my equipment!"

"No, sir."

Waiting on the porch for this latest intrusion to end, Jack shoved his hands into his back pockets and scowled at the steady stream of pickup trucks, cars, four-wheelers, bicycles and pedestrians on the puddle-spotted lane at the end of his driveway. Teenagers' car stereos thumped bass beats that vibrated the window glass, and shrill voices called excited greetings. Kyle Landry and his cousin, Tony, sold lemonade at the curve in the road. Sunset only seemed to increase the party atmosphere.

Jack's mouth twisted in disgust. All because a ditzy reporter didn't have sense enough to stick to the facts and leave the wild speculation to cheezy tabloids. And because of her, he'd been subjected to unadulterated chaos and countless interruptions. His calculations were off, his measurements were behind schedule and his evaluations were skewed. Concentration was impossible. Hell, he hadn't even been able to make an uninterrupted trip to the bathroom! And as far as eating or sleeping...

Now, that was a curious thing. Every time he'd been able to drop off, he'd dreamed of flashing railroad lights, or seen embers from old Boy Scout campfires flickering behind his closed eyelids. And then there was that incessant tapping. Had to be squirrels in the attic crawl spaces, crickets in the baseboards or something. Not that he was unduly concerned by things going bump in the night, but he guessed he was just a city boy at heart, because the country sure didn't live up to its reputation for peace and quiet—not by a long shot!

"Thanks, mister." The cheerful young man stepped off the porch, carrying Tommy piggyback.

"Don't mention it."

"You're a real lifesaver. Just wait'll I tell little sis—"

Jack gulped, feeling desperate. "Really, *don't mention it.*"

"We'll be back, mister."

"Oh, hell!"

Muttering, Jack ground his teeth in frustration, then stalked inside and scowled at the rows of beakers and technical equipment. Until he had ample time and quiet to ponder the latest calculations, he couldn't make a decision about the next step in his experiment. Maybe a change of scene would help him work out some details. At least things couldn't get any worse.

Three-quarters of an hour later, Jack hurled his fishing line into the bayou again, not even concerned that his new spinner hadn't attracted a single nibble. As he stood on the end of the pier, his mind floated somewhere in hyperspace amid a plethora of mathematical calculations and creative conjectures. Yes, there was a critical connection between algoids and water-oxygen ratios, and he teetered on the verge of knowing just what they were—

"Dr. Cooper! Oh, yoo-hoo!"

Jack jumped. A fish struck his line, spinning nylon thread out of his reel in a furious rush. And the bubble of comprehension he'd been oh-so-delicately wooing burst completely and was instantly lost. Cursing, he thumbed the reel and set the hook, then spun on this newest interloper with a snarl.

The pert-faced blonde in a crisp linen suit and high heels crossed the dock at a breakneck speed, her megawatt smile blinding him.

"Dr. Cooper. Kay Bennet from KJED, Lafayette. I wonder if I could have a word."

"Hold up there, Kay!" A movie-star-handsome man in a sport coat jogged down the dock after her. "I'd like to speak to you, too, Dr. Cooper!"

On the shoreline, a pair of cameramen carrying video equipment on their shoulders jostled for position.

"I saw him first, Jim!"

"All's fair in love and television, honey." The man stuck out his hand. "Jim Ferris, WBQD, Baton Rouge."

"Uh—" Jack's hands were busy with the furiously bucking fish on the end of his line.

The blonde glared at her competitor. "You're not going to scoop me this time, Ferris!"

"Oh, yeah? Watch this." He grinned and shoved a hand recorder in Jack's face. "Dr. Cooper, would you care to comment on the UFO sighting in Whiskey Bay?"

Not to be outdone, Kay Bennet dragged out her own microphone. "Dr. Cooper, is it true you're here on NASA's behalf? As a former mission specialist, what have you got to say about extraterrestrial life?"

"Have we really had a close encounter? What's the official government line?"

"Is the landing site legitimate or do you think it's a hoax?"

"Have you heard from Washington?"

"Is the FBI coordinating the investigation? The CIA?"

"What about—"

Questions bombarding him from all sides, Jack felt punch drunk. Damn! What the hell was going on? And how had these two TV news hounds known he was even here? There was only one person—

Jack suddenly understood, and his temper snapped. "Hold the damn phone!"

His roar silenced the reporters for an instant. Grim-lipped with rising fury, Jack cranked his reel, pulling a flopping nine-pound big mouth bass out of the water.

"That's a beauty," Jim Ferris said admiringly. He gestured toward one of the cameraman. "Yo, Carl! Be sure to get a shot of this whale! Hey, Doc! You think spaceship gamma radiations caused the thing to mutate? What about this lead—Fearless Astronaut Captures Monster Mutant Fish?"

"That does it!" Unhooking the bass, Jack abandoned his pole and tackle box. With his thumb hooked in the mouth of his prize fish, he stomped up the dock, trailing water and reporters.

"Just a few more questions, please—"

"No comment."

"Does that mean you *can't* comment?" the woman demanded with gleeful relish. "Then something really *is* going on!"

"No comment."

"Come, come, Doc!" Ferris was cajoling now. "Off the record, just tell me why you're here."

"Vacation," Jack snapped. Stepping off the dock, he dodged the pair of cameramen busily recording his every movement. He held up the bass. "Fishing, see?"

Ferris smirked and winked like a coconspirator. "Right. We see. Mum's the word, eh?"

"Dr. Cooper, my station is willing to bid for exclusive rights to your report." Kay Bennet's tone held a note of desperation.

Ferris scowled at her. "We'll double anything they offer!"

"You lowdown skunk! Why, I'll—"

"There's nothing to offer for," Jack said in disgust. "I'm not investigating anything!"

Kay Bennet snapped her head around, her expression expectant. "Then you've already made your determination? What conclusions did you—"

"We'll make you a better deal, Doctor," Ferris interrupted hastily. "Don't tell her a thing."

Kay Bennet glared at her adversary. "Butt out, Ferris!"

"Don't tell me what to do. I'm going to stick to the doc here like glue until I get to the bottom of this."

"Over my dead body!"

Nose to nose, the reporters wrangled over Jack like

dogs over a bone, but at least they'd forgotten him for the moment. Even the camera crew was filming the altercation. Scowling ferociously, Jack turned on his heel and stalked unnoticed into the underbrush, following the narrow trail bisecting the back of the Ballard estate.

Stick like glue, would they? Jack had been around enough reporters in his time to know they'd make a royal nuisance out of themselves until they got their stories. But not if he was nowhere to be found. Deprived of their quarry, they'd have to go after new game.

In the meantime, he knew exactly where this trail led, and he had a bone to pick with a certain big-mouthed redhead. Not only was she responsible for the three-ring circus currently on his doorstep, but Ciel Landry had betrayed a confidence, and he was going to take great delight in exacting his retribution out of her pale, freckled hide.

"SO WHEN LAUREN broke a second nail and started crying, I figured it was high time to close up shop for the day."

Shorts-clad legs tucked in her favorite wicker rocker on the sunporch at the rear of the Landry house, Marie nodded to her daughter. "Good thinking. I'd hate to have Tiny on my case, too."

Ciel flung her purse onto the matching wicker settee and heaved a tired sigh. Lush ferns hung on hooks around the porch, giving a tropical feel to the cluttered glassed-in room, and a small television droned in the background. The broad banks of windows revealed Marie's flower-filled backyard, bounded by the clapboard garage whose rickety exterior staircase gave access to the second-story storeroom Ciel had staked out as a home office.

"Honestly, Mama, can I help it if the phone's rung off the hook for two days?" She pressed her hands into the small of her back, stretching the tired muscles under her blouse and khaki skirt. "Lord, the whole town's gone nuts. Not that I'm complaining about all the activity, but I've never seen anything like it!"

"My, my, nor have I," Marie murmured appreciatively. "Ciel, do you know this young man?"

Ciel glanced up at the dark-haired, broad-shouldered silhouette looming in the doorway like a bad-tempered Sasquatch and gasped. "Jack."

"Not your astronaut!"

Ciel cast her mother a startled glance. "How'd you know—"

She choked to a stop, her stomach sinking. *Silly question. Mama always knows everything!*

At the sound of his knock, Marie rose from the rocker, making a shooing motion. "Don't just stand there—invite him in!"

Ciel dutifully opened the glass door, swallowing hard. The expanse of masculine chest in a thin white T-shirt was enough to give any woman major palpitations, but it was the ominous light in Jack Cooper's eyes that made her heart lurch to an absolute stop, then slam into warp drive. Breathless, she tried to smile.

"Well, hello. What brings you to our neck of the woods?"

"A pair of bloodthirsty journalistic piranhas. As if you didn't know."

Uh-oh. His growl raised the hairs on the back of Ciel's neck. She glanced at the gargantuan finned creature he held hooked between his thumb and forefinger. "Good Lord, where'd you get that? Loch Ness?"

Jack gave the bass a startled glance, almost as if he'd forgotten it was there. "Uh—"

Ciel had a sudden flash, and her smile became brilliant. "How sweet. You wanted to show off your catch. Didn't I tell you the fishing was great? Uncle Etienne always caught the prizewinning whoppers. Honestly, you'd think there was something strange in the water makes 'em grow so huge—"

"Don't you start," Jack warned. "It has nothing to do with gamma radiations."

Startled, she frowned. "Gamma? Hey, do you know Lincoln Dobbs?"

"Don't leave a guest standing on the stoop, *chère*," Marie admonished, bustling forward to usher Jack inside. "Come in, come in! I'm Ciel's mother."

Ciel made introductions while Marie admired the bass. "What a prize catch. Dare I hope it's for our supper?"

Jack hesitated, then thrust it toward her. "Ah, be my guest, ma'am."

Marie accepted the huge fish, delighted. "I'll get busy on it right away. You'll stay, won't you? So good to have you close by, Jack. I've known the Ballard family for absolute ages. You know, René's mother and I went to school together."

Jack looked a bit dazed. "Well, no, actually—"

"Oh, yes, and we keep in touch, you know. Talked just yesterday, as a matter of fact. Spoke highly of you, Jack. Mighty proud. Now, who did you say your people are?"

Hoping to avert Marie's well-meaning third degree, Ciel hastily intervened. "Jack's an air force brat, Mama."

"My, how fascinating." A door slammed and a

cheery "Yoo-hoo" sailed through the air. Marie hollered over her shoulder. "We're out back, Tee-Ta."

Tee-Ta Pearson, a plump bundle of Cajun mama who was a nearly identical match for her sister Marie except for her current platinum-blond dye job, flew into the sunroom. "Where's that Ciel? Lord, I been so worried about you, girl! Now, you just come here and let your Aunt Tee-Ta fix you up."

"Worried? But why?" Ciel asked, then frowned, perplexed by her aunt's strange getup, consisting of a metal headband attached by thick black cables to a battery pack, with dials slung around her neck.

"Because you aren't adequately protected, that's why!" Tee-Ta said in disgust, stripping off the instrument. "Not if you're out there investigating space aliens and UFOs like I hear tell!"

"Tee-Ta, whatever are you blabbering about?" Marie asked mildly.

"Prevention." Tee-Ta pushed the contraption into Ciel's hands, then started unslinging cords attached to various-sized crystal pendants from around her neck and placing them over Ciel's head. "That's a genuine Ace A-1 Alien Detector. Points 'em out at a hundred yards or more. Reads neutrinos or electrons or some such thing. Bought it at the hardware store, and it's got a money-back guarantee."

Ciel grinned. "So if I get abducted by extraterrestrials, you get a refund? That's reassuring."

Tee-Ta frowned sternly. "This is no time to make jokes. Promise me you'll wear it every day."

"But, Aunt Tee-Ta!"

"And these crystals, too. They may be old-fashioned, but Uncle Etienne always said they'd ward off everything from werewolves to athlete's foot, and you can't afford to take chances if you're out there calling attention to yourself poking around unexplained phenomena."

"Well, thank you," Ciel said, genuinely touched. She kissed her aunt's plump cheek. "That's really kind. And we were just telling Jack some of Uncle Etienne's giant fish stories."

"Jack? Oh, your astronaut." Tee-Ta ignored Jack's startled look. "Pleased to meet you. You know, Etienne was something of a space expert in his day, before his mind got so fuzzy."

"Is that so?"

"Yes, indeed. Used to write all sorts of pamphlets back in the forties and fifties about space visitors, moon shots, meteorites—things like that. Didn't much like the notoriety it caused, so he quit it in later years. I might be able to find some of them in the attic if you're interested."

"I'd like to see them, Aunt Tee-Ta," Ciel said.

"Sure thing, *chère*." Tee-Ta glanced at the fish her sister held. "Shouldn't you get that on ice?"

"We're going to have it for supper, courtesy of dear Jack," Marie said. "If you help me fillet it, I'll invite you to stay."

"You're on."

Marie and Tee-Ta headed for the kitchen. Ciel dropped the alien detector on a nearby table and gave Jack a smile. "Nothing like fresh fish for dinner. Thanks, Jack."

Sniffing his hands, he scowled, then ran his palms down the sides of his jeans. "Don't kid yourself that it was a peace offering. You've got a helluva lot of explaining to do."

"Me? About what?"

"For starters, that sideshow in front of my camp house. There're at least a thousand tourists marching up and down, all intent on seeing the bug-eyed aliens from Mars!"

"Now, hold on a minute," Ciel spluttered indignantly. "You can't blame that on me. I didn't tell a flying saucer to land in your front yard!"

"For crying out loud, there's no such thing as a flying saucer!"

"I think there very well could be, so there!"

"Well, that newspaper of yours has half the countryside convinced we've been invaded, and the other half is parading through my bathroom just for fun!"

Ciel bit her lip. Just her luck. For once, her prediction had been right on the money. "I can see how that might be...distracting for you."

"You don't know the half of it."

"But all I did was report the facts."

"In the most sensational fashion possible—and I'm paying the price in privacy and disrupted work. Lady, you're dangerous!"

A phone rang in the kitchen as Ciel's temper flared and her cheeks heated.

Jack continued. "The only thing I want to know—"

"Ciel, it's for you." Marie bustled into the sunroom, wiping her cornmeal-covered hands on her apron and thrusting her portable phone at her daughter. In a loud whisper, she said, "It's your boss."

"Oh, Lord." Ciel lifted the receiver to her ear. "Hello, Mr. Crenshaw? Oh, you saw this week's issue?"

Ciel winced and held the phone away from her ear as Roy Crenshaw barked his displeasure so loudly she was sure that Marie and Jack could hear every vitriolic syllable. After a minute, she broke through the tirade, trying to make her voice reasonable and businesslike.

"I know the *Press* isn't a scandal sheet, Mr. Crenshaw, but—what!" Her yelp rose an octave. "Shut us down? This week? No, sir, you can't! Why not? Because—"

Gulping in alarm, Ciel lifted her startled blue eyes to Jack's face. After his annoyance, she would have expected to see satisfaction at this terrible news, but what she saw was concern, quickly masked. A bolt of something potent, an instinctual certainty, gave her the strength to draw a deep breath, then speak forcefully.

"Ceasing publication would be a big mistake, Mr. Crenshaw. Monumental, in fact. Why do I say that? Because," she crowed, grinning, "thanks to that story, circulation has tripled, and we've already sold over three thousand dollars' worth of advertising for next week's UFO Moonlight Madness sale!"

4

"THANK GOD money talks—to Roy Crenshaw, any way." Ciel returned the telephone to her mother and blotted her damp forehead with the back of her shaking hand. "The *Press* gets a temporary reprieve. Not to mention my job."

"Cause for celebration." Marie beamed. "Let's break out that nice Chablis Tee-Ta gave me for Christmas, to go with Jack's fish."

Jack ducked his head to avoid a hanging fern. "Don't go to that trouble, Mrs. Landry, I can't—"

"No trouble at all," she said airily, bustling back toward the kitchen. "And call me Marie."

"Your mother listens as well as you do," Jack muttered.

"She's just happy I'm not out on my ear, but I guess you wouldn't understand."

Jack gave Ciel an exasperated glance. "Look, no one wants you to lose your job, but a UFO Moonlight Madness promotion just encourages more craziness. All the kooks and crackpots in the state have landed on my doorstep as it is. I can't get a damn thing done."

For all that he radiated so much masculine charisma she could hardly breathe, he deserved to be taken down a notch or two. "And craziness is in the eye of the beholder. There's a mysterious footprint in the rice field, or at least there was until it rained. Who's not to say we've had visitors from outer space? This could be another Roswell incident for all you know!''

''Which was never corroborated.'' Jack's lean features went stony with annoyance. ''As a scientist, I don't believe the little speck of dust we're sitting on warrants that kind of interest from a superior intelligence, even if one exists, which, in my humble opinion, is extremely unlikely.''

''Don't you believe in possibilities?''

''I'd rather stick to the facts.''

''You're a hard case, Professor. But let me tell you, some pretty odd things are happening around here.'' She ticked items off on her fingers. ''Sally Jessup's burglars. Three of Sam Holly's cows keeled over dead without a mark on them. Hazel Plinton's two-hundred-year-old oak lost every single leaf in one afternoon. And then there're those teenagers who spotted floating lights out on Cemetery Road and—''

''I get the picture.'' He looked at Aunt Tee-Ta's alien detector sitting on the wicker coffee table, then back pointedly at Ciel. ''Can I help it if this town has more lunatics per capita than any asylum?''

She perched her hands on her hips and tilted her chin in challenge. ''Scoff if you must, but this is not a normal Whiskey Bay summer. I mean, what if we have been visited by extraterrestrials and they're manipulating our thoughts somehow, making everyone act out of the ordinary?''

''It's the damn heat, that's all.''

''Ah, but what if the aliens just want us to *think* it's the heat so we won't get suspicious? Of course, a superior species could be manipulating the heat, too.''

''Are you aware of how nuts that sounds?''

''I've made a running list of unexplained phenomena

and odd human behavior, and it's getting impressively long.'' She prodded him, watching with great interest the rising flush staining his tanned cheeks. ''Where's your scientific curiosity? You could at least take a look at that rice field.''

''Uh, I already did,'' he admitted, then held up a hand at her expectant expression. ''And found nothing that couldn't be explained by natural phenomena. Probably some weird bacteria or something.''

''Cool!'' she said with as much sarcasm as she could muster.

''The explanation may be as simple as deer grazing in that field, Ciel.''

''Oh, yeah,'' she drawled, ''and Bambi just happened to chomp a perfect circle in the middle of it. And how many monkeys typing how many millennia before they chanced to write the Bible?''

''I have no doubt there's a reasonable explanation, but get this straight, *it wasn't a flying saucer.*''

''Yeah? Well, I'd like to prove you wrong, just to knock that smug look off your face, Professor.''

''How do you propose to do that?''

Her smile was lofty. ''An investigative reporter investigates. I'll find out the truth if it kills me. And then I'm going to shove the truth I discover straight down your skeptical throat.''

''Just remember the laws of nature don't lie. Not like a certain reporter who made a promise then ratted on me to the news media.''

Ciel gasped. ''I did not!''

''Then why were two television types breathing down my neck, assuming NASA sent me to investigate this ridiculous business?''

She shook her head. "I swear, Jack, I never said a word. It had to be Mama's doing."

He threw up his hands. "Oh, swell, blame your own mother!"

"I told you she has the best early-warning system in the nation, didn't I? And she said she talked with René's mom. You can bet she got everything down to whether you wear boxers or briefs under your space suit."

"You aren't serious?"

"As a heart attack." She glared at him. "Sorry to inform you, Jack, but if it's gone out on Mama's grapevine, then everybody in Whiskey Bay knows exactly who you are. Those TV people probably were the very last to get the scoop."

He groaned. "Good God."

She gave in to the impulse to goad him. "And folks will surely say if NASA is sending in a top man like you, then there must really be something going on with the flying saucer thing."

Aggravation made his tone as rough as gravel. "Nothing is going on."

"What's it hurt if folks learn about your being with NASA, anyway?"

He shoved a hand through his hair. "I've got my professional reputation to consider. Now, thanks to you, I'm associated with Whiskey Bay's lunatic fringe."

"I've never met anyone so paranoid and mistrustful!" She swallowed a sudden knot of emotion, and her words were tight. "I did not break my promise, you, you…!"

Throwing herself into Marie's rocker, she stared at the television screen and fought back tears.

"Oh, hell." Jack dropped to his haunches in front of her, frowning at her averted face. "You're not crying, are you?"

"Of course not." Her voice was suspiciously watery. "That might imply I care what you think. Which I certainly do not."

Resting his hands on the rocker's arms, he heaved an exasperated sigh. "Maybe I did jump to conclusions...."

"Jump? You leaped that tall building with a single bound, rocket man."

"If I've misjudged you, I apologize."

"*If?*" Eyes swimming, Ciel glared at him. "Why don't you just go home and cuddle up with your raccoons and microscopes, Professor? And while you're at it, you can..."

Jack leaned forward, bottling up whatever else she might have said with the electric pressure of his mouth over hers.

Shock mingled with pleasure to chase every thought from Ciel's brain, leaving only a flood of sensation. The warmth of his lips. The unique flavor of his mouth. The scent of him—slightly salty and with a tang of piney after-shave—filling her nostrils.

When the raspy tip of his tongue pressed insistently against the seam of her lips, she shivered uncontrollably, opening for his invasion without conscious volition, surrendering to the thrill of his tender possession. Somehow, his hands were in her hair, holding her still, even though she hadn't moved, and his tongue twined with hers in wicked ways.

Nothing could have prepared her for his skillful wooing, the subtleties of his lips mastering hers, leaving her breathless and trembling. The attraction she'd felt from their first encounter had done nothing to forewarn her of his power, and she knew that whatever else he accused her of, he was many times more dangerous to her peace of mind than she could ever be to his. And that knowledge made her tremble anew.

Jack raised his head, his lips still brushing hers, the tip of his tongue testing the sensitive corners of her mouth. He dragged her fingertips down to examine her delicate jawbone, and his voice was a rumble of masculine hunger.

"Didn't I tell you that mouth of yours would get you in trouble?"

"What?" Dazed, dizzy, she could hardly lift her eyelids, but then the sense of what he'd said, what he'd done, slammed through her. She was appalled; her eyes flew open wide and she jerked to her feet, nearly tipping Jack over.

"Whoa, there." Scrambling to his feet, he reached for her again.

Totally unnerved, not only by the man but by the potency of her own response, Ciel snatched the alien detector from the coffee table, flipped on switches and pointed it at Jack like a weapon. "Back off, flyboy!"

"Now, Ciel..."

"I'm onto your tactics, Dr. Cooper," she hissed, furious. The gizmo in her hands beeped in protest and the dials leaped into the red zones. "You're just like all men, thinking you can run roughshod over a woman's feelings and then simply kiss it better. Well, forget it! Now, get out."

"Or what? You'll zap me with your ray gun?"

His expression told her how ludicrous she looked, but she was too rattled to back off. "If it was good enough for Princess Leia..."

"Fine." The muscle in his jaw jerked. "If that's the way you want it, I'm out of here."

"Fine. Give my regards to your raccoons."

With a last glance that might have held an element of regret—or worse, vast relief, Ciel couldn't be certain—Jack stormed out the rear door and vanished into the backyard gloom. Shaken, Ciel plopped down again in the wicker rocker and tossed the detector aside.

Marie poked her head out of the kitchen. "That wasn't Jack I heard leaving, was it? And supper's almost ready! Why'd you let him go, *chère?*"

"Ah, he had a pressing engagement with a jar of pond scum."

Marie made a clucking sound, shaking her head. "Scientists. Who can figure them?"

Not me. Ciel swallowed and clasped one of the crystal pendants in her palm, praying it was also a charm against foolish lovesickness. It was abundantly clear that the last thing she needed in her life was a wary, suspicious man like Jack Cooper, someone who was only going to be around for a short time anyway, and whose stuck-in-the-mud, too-conventional attitude meant he'd never be able to cut loose and enjoy life to its fullest. Not without help, anyhow.

Ciel stifled a little moan of distress. Logic and clear thinking and knowing what it took to avoid trouble were all well and good, but those qualities had never been her strong suit. If she was smart, she'd concentrate on her investigation and try to forget that a certain man's kisses were out of this world.

She sighed. Proving the existence of alien visitors suddenly seemed a whole lot easier than that.

"Hold still, Tiny. I'm trying to focus."

"Hurry up, Ciel. These things make me nervous."

Ciel peered through the camera's viewfinder at Tiny Herbert's impressive bulk, now dwarfed by a foreboding twelve-foot high wall of tangled, undulating plant life creeping out of the woods into Tiny's cultivated fields. Anything that intimidated a man of Tiny's size and strength was worth paying attention to.

"Me, too," she muttered, tripping the shutter button. "It's right out of *Day of the Triffids*. Okay, all done."

Biceps bulging under his cotton T-shirt, Tiny pulled his baseball cap back on his mahogany curls and stepped gratefully away from the towering mass of twisted tendrils and sinisterly succulent fronds. "Just like *Jack and the Beanstalk*, huh?"

Ciel flipped open her notebook. "Appeared overnight, you say?"

"Practically. Lauren noticed it first."

"You sure you didn't accidentally dump an extra load of fertilizer around here?"

"No, I didn't."

"What is it, anyway? Got any idea?"

"Looked it up in my old college ag books. Best I can figure, it's got to be first cousin to one of those trap plants. Look at the teeth on that blossom, will you?"

"Teeth?" Ciel's eyes got wide. "Trap?"

"You know, it catches bugs and dissolves 'em with acid."

"A Venus flytrap?"

"Yes." Tiny cast a worried glance at the vegetation and a shudder rippled his bronzed hide. "Only, this one's a man-eater."

"GET YER JAMBALAYA right here!"

"Horace, get that Popsicle out of your sister's ear!"

"Sister Inez, the All-Seeing. Palm readings discounted to five bucks!"

Wide-eyed, Ciel muttered, "Holy cow jumped over the moon!"

In search of a front-page picture for next week's *Press,* she clutched her camera and pressed through the crush of Saturday-afternoon curiosity seekers moving up and down the tent city mushrooming on the grassy shoulders of Ballard Road. In the steamy August heat, her jeans and striped shirt clung to her damp skin. The scents of grilled onions and cotton candy drifted from concessionaires in wheeled trailers with pop-out countertops. Young mothers pushing strollers vied with tourists in Bermuda shorts and sandals for elbow room.

"Hey, honey!" An enterprising huckster in one of the many canvas-roofed crafts booths lining the congested road hoisted a T-shirt with a logo that read I Survived the Invasion of Whiskey Bay. "Better get one now. They're going fast!"

Ciel laughed and shook her head. "Not today, thanks."

The man held up a handmade quilt and a fistful of alligator belts. "Then take hubby something. For you, twenty percent off!"

Ciel waved him away, then dodged a Greyhound bus with New Orleans plates edging its way through the bumper-to-bumper traffic. With a hydraulic hiss, the bus disgorged an energetic tour guide keeping up a steady flow of description in a language Ciel couldn't begin to identify and several dozen Asian travelers carrying video cameras. They stampeded for the observation point, a lookout over the flat expanse of terraced rice fields marked by multicolored gas station pennants strung up on cane fishing poles.

"Don't enter there, sister!" A bearded man in a white clerical robe grabbed Ciel's arm. He wore a placard that said Repent, The End Is Near. "It's the devil's work! Sing with me now, 'We shall gather at the river-r-r...'"

"Sorry, I can't carry a tune in a tin bucket," Ciel said, pulling free. Farther up the road, she caught sight of Deputy Cleveland Henderson directing traffic. "Excuse me, Reverend. Hey, Cleveland! How's it going?"

The deputy waved an ancient, rusty tanker truck with a Prejean Oil logo on its side through an almost too-narrow gap in the traffic. As it sped off in a cloud of dust toward the company's isolated work yard a few miles down the road, the harried officer flashed Ciel a big grin. "It's a zoo!"

"I'll say." Dumbfounded by the carnival-like tumult—Mardi Gras, the Fourth of July and New Year's Eve all rolled into one—Ciel felt guilt prick her conscience. No wonder Jack Cooper was ticked off. All this furor for the sake of a little flattened rice field!

"Listen, Cleveland, did the sheriff ever hear back about those lab reports?"

"Yeah, but nothing conclusive. And now, what with that rain and all this trampling around..." The deputy shrugged. "Guess we'll never know what caused that thing out there."

The reporter in Ciel couldn't settle for that, but before she could say so, a horn bleated at her heels. Startled, Ciel scrambled sideways to avoid the fender of a late-model Cadillac. The driver was Emile Nabors, looking as bad tempered as ever despite windows rolled up to contain the car's air-conditioning.

"I hope you're satisfied!" he shouted through the glass.

Irritated, Ciel cupped her ear with her palm and made her expression blank. "Can't hear you, Emile."

Punching a power button, he rolled the window down

on the passenger side, and the car exhaled a rush of cool air into Ciel's heated face. "I said I hope you're satisfied with this fine mess you've made!"

"Oh, you flatterer, Emile!" She giggled demurely, a picture of fetching modesty. "Why, Mr. Nabors, I'd never presume to take all the credit for this wonderful event."

"Wonderful? We've practically got a riot on our hands! Do you have any idea what all this police overtime is costing the town?"

Ciel stifled a sigh. There were always those who saw the glass as half empty instead of half full. In Ciel's estimation, however, Emile's irritation over the UFO furor was out of proportion to any real problem.

"Count your blessings, Mayor," she advised, her lips twisting with mischief. "What you've got here is Whiskey Bay's First Annual Impromptu UFO Festival."

"That's a ridiculous notion," he spluttered.

"Is it? Look at all these people having fun. I must say that it's certainly more organized and better attended than anything we've ever had before, especially that Fruit Fest idea of yours a couple of years ago." Ciel grinned at him, loving the way his ears were turning red. "I ask you, who wants to celebrate plums and peaches? Nobody, that's who."

Emile punched the window button and set his car in motion again, sending Ciel a final glare that was pure venom. "There's just no reasoning with you, you—"

Thankfully, the closing glass muffled his insult.

Her mouth compressed with anger, Ciel took a quick picture, thinking Emile's profile would look perfect on the post office's Most Wanted board. "Same to you, Emile. Can I quote you on that?"

Slinging her camera over her arm, Ciel waved goodbye to Cleveland, then trudged up the track, dodging college students in cutoffs and grandmothers with parasols. She finally reached a card table surrounded by ice chests from which two adolescent budding entrepreneurs were selling cups of green liquid their hand-lettered sign identified as Alien Blood.

"Hey, boys. How's business?"

Kyle looked up from making change and dipping ice. "Great! The little kids love this stuff."

"Yeah, we're making a mint," Tony agreed, pouring the concoction from a gallon milk jug into a line of waiting cups. "Wanna try some? On the house for relatives."

"Thanks." Ciel thirstily downed a cup. "Um, good. Tastes like lemonade."

"You're not supposed to tell," Kyle protested. "Anyway, it's the secret ingredient that's important. Show her, Tony."

Tony held up a small plastic vial of green food coloring. "The only beverage with its own special effects. Gives the customers an alien tongue."

"What!" Ciel stared at the cup she held in mock horror. "You hoodlums, why didn't you warn me? Is my tongue green?"

Kyle nodded, grinning. "Emerald."

"No, more like kelly," Tony hazarded.

"Not the fashion statement I wanted to make today," Ciel groaned. "Too late now, I suppose."

"Hey, Ciel, you know what to do with a green alien, don't ya?" Kyle asked.

"No, what?"

He smirked. "Wait until it gets ripe."

"A candidate for 'Star Search' you're not," she declared. "Anyway, Mama wants to know if you fellows need anything. More ice? How about some—"

"Look, here he goes again." Tony pointed to a tan van coming up the road.

"Think he'll make it this time?" Kyle asked.

"Nah."

Ciel frowned at the familiar vehicle. "That's Jack—er, Dr. Cooper."

"Yeah, did you know he used to be a real space shuttle astronaut?"

"After that TV news report the other night, I suppose everyone does," Ciel said, sighing.

"I'll say! Watch this." Kyle pointed as several onlookers shouted and waved at the van attempting to reach the lane leading down to the bayou camp house. "Last time he tried to get to Uncle Etienne's place he had to sign about a zillion autographs before they'd let him through."

"Oh, boy."

Sure enough, a crowd of admirers blocked Jack's progress, filling up the road in front of the van while they snapped photos, rapped on the van's windshield and held out napkins and check stubs for his signature. Jack leaned out the window, scribbling madly, doing his best to be accommodating while still inching forward—the only choice under the circumstances—but even from this distance Ciel could see his pained expression.

Another twinge of guilt lodged under her breastbone. While she wouldn't take full responsibility for his plight, she would admit that she might have stirred things up just a tad.

"Mama says close up shop by sundown, boys." Inspecting the gauntlet of excited tourists, Ciel squared her shoulders. "I'd better go rescue Jack."

"He's an astronaut," Kyle protested. "Nerves of steel. Plenty of guts. Guys like that don't need rescuing!"

"That's what you and he both think." Humming a few bars of Elton John's "Rocket Man," Ciel set off.

When she reached the bottleneck, she pulled her press pass from her wallet and waded through the mass of humanity crowding Jack's van. "Okay, break it up. Let me through. Official press business!"

The crowd parted momentarily, and Ciel hopped onto the van's front bumper.

Jack leaned out of the window. "Ciel, what the hell—"

"Shut up and drive, Professor." She motioned forward. "Wagons, ho!"

The crowd laughed good-naturedly and stepped aside, and Jack bounced the van up the road, turned into the lane and finally pulled up in front of the camp. Ciel scrambled off the bumper, breathless. "Were you trying to shake me loose from my fillings?"

"Sorry." Grim-mouthed, he killed the engine, grabbed a plastic grocery bag from behind the seat and got out of the van. "But when you're breaking orbit, it's throttles at full or you're liable not to make it at all."

She gave him a sympathetic look. "That bad, huh?"

"You can see for yourself."

And indeed she could.

Remnants of orange plastic tape that he'd tried to use to indicate parking areas hung in tatters between cypress trees. The No Trespassing signs were universally ignored. Up and down the lane, people were tailgating off their pickup trucks, picnic baskets open, charcoal burning in their hibachis, lawn chairs out. Families lounged on blankets; teenage girls in bikinis sunned themselves on beach towels; and behind the camp a bevy of fisherman lined the pier.

"They're like rabbits," Jack muttered. "I turn my head and they multiply."

"At least everyone seems friendly," Ciel offered.

"Yeah, friendly enough to count my bathroom as their own and bring me jars of pickled okra and borrow cups of sugar I need for my experiments, for God's sake!" He scowled. "I'm thinking of getting a Doberman."

"Jack! You wouldn't!"

"Don't push me, lady. Something with teeth is mighty appealing at the moment." With Ciel on his heels, he stomped up the porch and into the kitchen cluttered with beakers of green foamy goo and pieces of scientific equipment.

"Well, just stay inside and don't answer the door," she suggested reasonably.

"Tried it. First they drove me crazy knocking, then they starved me out." Opening the sack, he unloaded a package of chocolate cupcakes, half a dozen individual bags of pretzels and pistachio nuts, a six-pack of imported beer and a gripper bag with three red pickled eggs.

"Starved? You mean you're out of supplies and that's all the groceries you got?" She eyed his purchases with disdain. "Don't you scientific types know anything about nutrition?"

Jack's mouth formed a sour curl. "There wasn't much of a selection at Barney's 7-Eleven, and since I was already beginning to draw a crowd, I was lucky to get this!"

Ciel inspected him. Circles lay under his eyes, and a day's growth of beard shadowed his lean jaw. His well-worn jeans and threadbare T-shirt looked like the last things out of a suitcase, but what they did for his male physique sent her libido into overdrive. His dark hair fell over his forehead in a fashion that made her fingers itch to smooth it back. Altogether, it was a sexy and appealingly vulnerable package of strung-out, exasperated, bone-tired masculinity.

And he was utterly irresistible, especially for a girl who suddenly couldn't remember why he'd made her angry their last meeting, but had no trouble at all remembering the man's passionate kisses.

Ciel bit her tingling lips, feeling guiltier than ever. "You do look a bit ragged."

"Try wiped out. I'll have to go back to Houston if this keeps up, but I've got some things cooking that shouldn't be moved, and I've lost enough time already...." Popping the flip top, he swigged the beer and reached for an egg. "Hell, I'm never going to make my deadline."

"Oh, no, don't say that!" Contrition clogged her throat. Unable to help herself, she reached out to touch his strong forearm in comfort. His tanned skin was seductively warm, the fine dark hairs silky. "I can't bear to think of that happening."

"I'm having to work at night to get anything done, but it's impossible to sleep during the day. Of course, I couldn't sleep at night anyway because the raccoons like to tap dance on the verandas and there's some sort of swamp gas on the bayou that keeps flickering like a flashlight."

Ciel's attention sharpened. "Or like Tinkerbell?"

"Well, I guess..." He reached for a second egg.

"Jack, that sounds just like Sally Jessup's case," she said excitedly. "This is great! You're both having the same kind of close encounter! Hey, I wonder if Uncle

Etienne ever noticed anything like this. We could go see him and—''

He scowled as a soft drumming began at the back door. ''This isn't an episode of 'The Outer Limits,' so don't start that nonsense again! This is where we got off track last time.''

''Okay. Okay. Aren't you going to answer the door? Someone's there.''

''Again. Yeah, I know.'' He stalked to the door, swung it open and barked, ''What?''

The back porch was empty. Frowning, Jack peered up and down the veranda, scanned the backyard, then shrugged. ''Third time that's happened. Must be that some plumbing in the attic sets up sympathetic vibrations in the door facings.''

''Must there be a logical explanation for everything with you?'' she demanded in exasperation. Jeez, the man had a Dead Zone where his imagination should be! ''Isn't it conceivable—''

''Not for one minute do I think I'm having visitors from Zork.'' Jack raised one eyebrow. ''But I do have a question for you, Ciel.''

Trepidation that he was going to take her to task for her part in his troubles made her wary. ''What's that?''

''Why is your mouth green?''

She blinked. ''Uh, alien blood.''

He snorted in disgust. ''Never a straight answer when a joke will do, right?''

''No, really.'' She clutched his arm. ''It's from Kyle's green lemonade. And yours is red. Your mouth, that is.''

His gaze dropped to her lips, and the air crackled with a sudden surge of sexual heat.

''Interesting condition,'' he murmured. ''Wonder what we should do about it.''

Ciel's tongue darted out, slicking her lips with moisture, her words a husky whisper. "It'll rub off after a while."

"Maybe we should experiment with accelerating the process." Cupping her chin, he lifted her mouth to his and rubbed his lips lightly over hers, sending shivers down every extremity. "It doesn't seem to be working."

With a sigh, Ciel slid her arms around his neck. "Maybe we should try harder."

He obliged, pulling her to him and taking her mouth completely. The stubble on his cheeks rasped her sensitive skin, underscoring their essential and exciting differences. His mobile tongue bewitched her senses, teasing and exploring and sending her reeling. Lost in pleasure, Ciel could feel her heart pounding in her chest, the rhythm a shuddering counterpoint to another, more intrusive, noise.

Reluctantly, Jack raised his head. "Hell, it's the front door now." Releasing her, he dragged a hand through his hair, his expression rueful. "Sorry, the story of my life these days."

For the first time, Ciel truly understood his frustration, for it matched her own. And she did feel just a teensy-weensy bit responsible for his predicament. Inspiration dawned, and she beamed up at him.

"Jack, I've got a great idea!"

"Oh, yeah?" Instant wariness narrowed his eyes.

"You need a quiet place to work, right? There's a room over our garage I use as an office. The wiring shorts out occasionally, but other than that, it's fully equipped, quiet. You can come and go as you please, check things over here when you have to, hole up there and work to your heart's content without any interruptions. Do you want it?"

For a moment he looked tempted, then shook his head. "Uh, that's probably not a good idea."

Because you just kissed me senseless? Ciel wondered. Was he so wary of entanglements he'd risk his own project? Well, she couldn't allow such mule-headed stubbornness!

"Look, I guarantee no one will bother you. You'll get *tons* of work done. Besides, what other choice do you have?"

"Hello?" a voice called from outside. The knocking came louder and more persistent than ever. "Anybody home? Junior's done set the portable toilet afire and we need a water hose!"

Jack rolled his eyes to heaven. "All right, Ciel. You've got a deal. Anything has to be better than this!"

5

"LOOKS LIKE a trash-can lid to me."

"No, a lamp shade."

"Frisbee."

"Weather balloon."

"So how'd it change colors like that?"

"Beats the heck out of me."

"Could you replay it, Harlan?" Ciel asked, chewing the tip of her pen.

Harlan Turner punched the rewind button on the VCR sitting on the counter in his barbershop, then pushed play. The members of the old-timers' club who daily frequented the shop—usually to watch their favorite soap opera without their wives' knowledge—leaned closer, peering over bifocals, squinting to see. On the television screen, an illuminated disk spun in a starlit sky.

"Your Lucy took this, Harlan?" Ciel asked.

"Right off our back porch. Scared the bejesus out of the old girl, but she's a trooper, she is. Stayed right on it with that camera we brought to film the grandkids until the dern thing up and disappeared."

"It's fantastic," Ciel breathed.

"Yeah, but is it real?" one of the customers demanded. "Still say it looks like a Frisbee."

"No Frisbee ever acted like that, friend."

"And don't you be doubting my Lucy's word, or I'll bust you a good'un," Harlan said heatedly.

"I'd like to speak to her," Ciel said.

"Sorry, Ciel. She ain't talking about it."

"But why?"

Harlan scratched his balding head. "Well, Lucy says it's one thing to be crazy. It's a whole 'nother thing to have the whole town know it!"

"SAY CHEESE!"

"Cheese!"

Ciel snapped the shutter and looked up at the city sanitation crew in their best bib and tucker as they stood in front of a large flatbed truck. "That's got it, fellows. Thanks!"

"Make sure you spell our names right, Ciel," one of the men called.

She tapped her notebook. "Got it all right here, Raymond. I guess this proves Whiskey Bay is moving into the twenty-first century."

"Highest technology available." Raymond hoisted himself into the truck, and the rest of the crew clambered aboard the tailgate. "As many tourists we got these days out at Ballard Road, I just hope twenty-five will be enough."

"I'm sure they'll bring a great deal of relief. Good luck!"

She waved as they pulled away, smiling at the bright-blue portable toilets piled high on the flatbed. Yes, sir. The town of Whiskey Bay wanted only the best for its visitors, especially those spending dollars. And now Jack's plumbing would finally get a rest!

JACK TURNED BACK to the computer screen, absently scanning the data base filled with his statistics. Outside the arched window of Ciel's tiny upstairs garage office, yet another Landry Friday-evening commotion enveloped the yard. Cars with Ciel's brothers and sisters were whizzing in; Kyle and Tony went shrieking by on their bicycles; while Mama Marie was hurrying out with a steaming casserole for some lucky neighbor.

He'd spent a week camping out on the office daybed, and the family dynamics still mystified him. Considering the constant uproar, plus the countless offers by Ciel and her mother of sustenance, gossip, typewriter ribbons, newspapers and clean laundry, he had almost as many interruptions as back at the camp!

He pushed aside a stack of fat manila folders, floppy disks and reference manuals, rubbed his tired eyes and rose from the computer desk.

Well, not quite that.

Thanks to Ciel's Moonlight Madness promotions, the interest in the Whiskey Bay "sighting" was still at a high and the crowds of tourists, pilgrims and crackpots were undiminished. Nevertheless, he was beginning to finally accomplish something with his project. If he could avoid any more interruptions, just focus on the problem...

Admit it, Cooper. Your main problem isn't mathematical. It's hormonal! A certain smart-aleck Venus with a peachy mouth was driving him slap out of his mind!

A strictly "hands off" policy and more cold showers than was good for a man hadn't helped, because every time Ciel rocketed into his vicinity with her generous, giving spirit and vibrant sunniness, he was hard pressed to remember that they just weren't suited. But that didn't change the fact that equations and algae and a chance to swelter in a Brazilian jungle couldn't hold a candle to

the fantasies that kept popping into his head about play-
ing dot to dot with the freckles on her creamy skin.

He groaned at the erotic image. *Get a grip, Cooper.*

"Jack?"

The object of his thoughts poked her curly head inside
the office door. Her expression was vaguely alarmed.

"I thought I heard—are you feeling okay?"

"Uh, fine." Jack swallowed hard.

In a clingy floral knit dress that exposed an enticing
amount of cleavage and long, slim legs, Ciel appeared
cool and delectable, and everywhere he tried not to look,
there were those darned freckles! He shoved his hands
into his back pockets and cleared his throat. "Just, uh,
thinking out loud."

She smiled brightly. "Well, in that case, would you
mind if I pulled a couple of things up on the computer
and printed out a hard copy to edit? I'll be as quick and
quiet as a mouse, I promise."

Jack felt a stab of guilt. Tightly focused on his goals,
he'd forgotten she had projects of her own. He went over
to the computer and saved his data onto a disk. "Of
course. This is your place. I was taking five anyway.
Working on the book?"

"Great." Rapidly, she selected her disk out of a file
box, popped his out and hers in, then went to work. The
printer began spitting out pages. "And yeah, I've ne-
glected Sylvie too long and she's griping at me."

"What's she up to?"

"Saving the universe, as usual."

"Seems to run in this family. Is that why you left a
city job?" Hip propped on the corner of the cluttered
desk, he nodded at a print of Atlanta on the wall signed
with goodbye messages from the staff of a large daily
paper.

"Oh, that." She shrugged, her expression flustered. "Well, I was an intern when Papa was killed offshore, and Mama needed me."

"You ever miss it?"

For a moment her sapphire eyes were wistful. There was a longing in her he recognized in himself, but also a loyalty that kept her steady in her purpose. There was a lot to admire in a woman like that.

With a shake of her head, she denied any lingering regret, and the corner of her shapely mouth tilted in wry humor. "Whiskey Bay may not always provide as much adventure as Atlanta or your South American rain forest, but it does have its moments."

Jack chuckled. "You've got that right."

"And besides, I've got Sylvie's interstellar travels to provide me with some excitement."

Jack's one-track brain immediately produced a picture of the kind of excitement he'd like to experience personally with her. His attempt to quash the notion failed miserably.

"There, all done! I'm sorry I interrupted you." She scooped up the manuscript pages and disks, then rose to her feet.

He felt strangely reluctant to see her go. "By the way, have you or the boys been to the camp while I was gone? Inside?"

"Of course not. Kyle and Tony wouldn't dare! Why?"

"Nothing, just some of my things—clothes, fishing gear—have been moved."

Her eyes widened in alarm. "Stolen?"

"No, nothing's missing, just rearranged, as if someone was curious and just took a look." He shrugged. "I locked up, but I guess some of those infernal tourists are responsible. They're polite, I have to give that to them—but they're getting too damned bold.''

She gave him a troubled look. "Lights, noises, now this. Jack, that's too many weird things happening to one man to be natural.''

"And your imagination is always working overtime.''

"Maybe so, but if you'd just open your eyes, you'd see that things aren't normal right now in Whiskey Bay!''

"Not that they ever were,'' he muttered.

"Suit yourself, Professor!'' With a haughty stare, she whipped around the corner of the desk on her way to the door, but banged her hip and sent the leaning tower of manila files toppling.

"Whoops!'' Ciel grabbed for the flying files, flinging half of them across the room, spewing pages onto the tile floor along with the box of black computer disks, Jack's paperwork and her newly printed manuscript pages.

"Oh, no!'' she gasped. "I'm sorry!'' Red-faced with chagrin, she fell to her knees, scraping and scrambling through the messy pile.

Despite the fact that shuffling his data was nothing short of a minor disaster, he might have laughed if her distress hadn't been so heartfelt. But how could he be angry when her glorious hair was falling loose about her shoulders and her posture revealed the mysterious shadowy hollow between her breasts?

"Don't worry about it.'' He dropped to one knee beside her, reaching for the clutter. She batted his hands away, stuffing disks into her pockets, gathering up files and papers and stacking them haphazardly on the desk top.

"No, don't touch a thing. I'll do it. Lord, why does

this always happen to me? I'm as clumsy as Godzilla strolling through Tokyo!''

He caught her wrists to stop her frantic gathering, and his voice was thick. ''Believe me, no one would ever mistake you for Godzilla.''

Bending his head, he fastened his mouth to hers, groaning with the sweetness of it. She sighed in welcome, opening for him fully, without equivocation or coyness, and he was instantly lost, tossed into a maelstrom of sensation.

Kneeling on the floor, he gathered her to him, his hand in the tender curve of her back. She was lithe and utterly female, and fit him as no woman ever had, every nuance and curve made with infinite perfection just for him. She leaned into him, kissing him back, her tongue nimble and enticing.

There was nothing beyond this moment, this woman. Drunk on her taste, Jack lifted her and carried her to the daybed, pressing her back against the star-studded quilt. He kissed her over and over, insinuating his knee between her legs, letting her feel the power of his need. Her response shattered him. She wrapped her arms around his neck, caressing the soft hairs on his nape, melting beneath his weight as if she'd been waiting an eternity to find him.

Groaning, Jack tasted the fine skin behind her earlobe, trailed hot kisses down the slender column of her neck, then lifted his hands to open buttons. Freeing the center clasp on her lacy bra, he exposed her lush, rose-tipped breasts to his heated gaze. The smattering of sandy freckles on her ivory skin enchanted him. He drew a shaky breath.

''God, you're lovely. Out of this world lovely.''

''Jack...''

Her fingers clenched his shoulders through his T-shirt, and he needed no further urging. He bent to lave the tender swells with his tongue, smiling against her skin as she shuddered with pleasure. When his lips circled the pebbled nub of her nipple, she convulsed, arching her back and sinking her hands into his dark hair.

He was without mercy, nipping at her with his teeth, loving what he could do to her, what she did to him. He was intoxicated by the scent of her, the way her full breast fit into his palm. Her hands were under his shirt, skimming through the bramble of chest hair, exploring the planes of his abdomen, probing boldly beneath the waistband of his jeans.

Jack's heart thundered, and he teetered on the brink of his control. Sinking his hands into her hair, he wrenched his mouth free and smiled wolfishly into her beautiful, dazed face.

"Isn't this reality better than any fantasy? Give up on those notions about little green men and invaders from Mars, Ciel. I've got better things for you right here on Earth."

Something flickered behind her blue eyes, darkened them to the color of storm clouds, and her voice shook. "Everything it seems except respecting my opinions."

He laughed, rubbing his lips over hers affectionately. "They're wild and adorable, but you can't be serious."

"You may think they're totally off-the-wall, but they're *mine,* and I'm entitled to them," she said on a soft, hurt gasp. Her hands came up to shove at his chest. "And if you'd just listen to what's going on, open your eyes—"

"I haven't got time or energy to waste on foolishness."

Her voice went rusty. "Is that all I am? Foolishness?"

"Uh-oh. Houston, we have a problem." He knew instantly he'd made a cosmic blunder. More than one.

"Ciel, I didn't mean…"

Hair in a wild tangle, she stared up at him accusingly. "I'm a believer, Jack. Are you?"

He hesitated. "No. I guess not."

"And never the twain shall meet." A peachy tide flooded her face, and she rolled from beneath him, tugging at her garments.

"Excuse me, I think I just avoided a big mistake."

Then she was gone, clattering down the staircase.

Jack got to his feet. As hard landings went, this was a lulu. He could have kicked himself, not just for opening his stupid mouth at a critical instant, but for hurting her. For a wild moment, he'd lost his natural caution, selfishly indulging in all that Ciel could give. She was more than dangerous; she was terrifying. She'd taken his hard-won control and dismantled it utterly with the merest touch of her hands and lips. For a man who prided himself on his self-discipline and dignified reserve, it was quite a blow.

Worse, she evoked in him a welter of unaccustomed and unwelcome emotions—guilt and lust and longing— things he'd thought he'd put behind him with Retha's desertion. Ciel was the sweetest thing he'd come across in this planetary system, but he wasn't looking for anything serious. No, he'd been down that path and knew it for the trap it was, but it was clear that Ciel wanted, needed, even deserved, more than a brief affair. Even though the chemistry between them was dynamite, it would be grossly unfair to her to take what they generated to its inevitable conclusion, no matter how badly he wanted her.

"WHAT'S THE MATTER, Charlie?"

"Listen." Sitting in the noonday sun on the curb in front of the *Press* office, Charlie Reynolds reached into a box and pulled out a can of root beer. Dozens of opened cans stood in regimental lines in the gutter. He popped the top. "Hear that?"

"Hear what?" Ciel asked.

"Exactly." Charlie's face hung in sad folds like a hound dog's. "No pop. No fizz. They're dead, Ciel. Every last one of them."

"Are you sure?"

"Positive. I opened 144 of 'em in the warehouse. All dead." His voice was mournful. "And they were fine yesterday."

Ciel frowned, scribbled a note in her notebook, then touched his shoulder in sympathy. "I'm sorry for your loss, Charlie. But won't they feed my geraniums just the same?"

"Can't risk it. Contaminated, you know."

"Then we'll have to go to plain water."

Charlie jumped to his feet in alarm. "No, ma'am! Something's in it these days. You want to end up like Lincoln Dobbs?"

"Hmm, you've got a point." She dug in her purse and handed him some bills. "Here, get what you need."

"Thanks, Ciel!" He cheered instantly, but as he turned away, heading for the corner store, he gave her warning. "Remember, don't drink the water!"

"DON'T TELL the warden."

Etienne Ballard winked, drew two twisty red licorice whips from the bag Ciel had just given him, then stuffed the package underneath the plump cushion of his wooden porch rocker. He had the face and hair of an eighty-year-old Einstein and sported small, oval Sergeant Pepper spectacles.

"It's just between you and me," Ciel said, with a laugh.

She settled into a matching rocker on the shady, pseudoantebellum veranda of the Harbor Home Retirement Center. There was a breath of cool on the early-morning air, and she drank it in gratefully, knowing it wouldn't last.

Maybe the blasted heat was only an excuse, but it was the only thing that explained her crazy impulses and crazier notions these days. Such as being more than halfway convinced extraterrestrials were in the vicinity. Such as being entirely too susceptible to the attraction of a dark-haired, relationship-shy scientist.

Etienne passed one licorice whip to Ciel, then sank his impossibly white, straight false teeth into his own and sighed. "Ah, breakfast of champions."

Ciel nibbled the sweet candy. "Sure it won't upset your blood sugar, Uncle Etienne?"

"Live dangerously, I always say. Only way to get a rush at my age."

"You old scoundrel!" She shook her head, then reached into her bag and pulled out half a dozen garishly printed pamphlets yellowed with age. "Listen, Aunt Tee-Ta found these for me. Can you tell me about them?"

Etienne took the pamphlets, held them up one by one in his gnarled hands.

Flying Saucers Identified.

Meteorites—Friends or Foes?

Moon Men and Their Dogs.

Comets and Comments—A Sourcebook for the Fifties.

Where the Cows Come Home: A Visit to the Milky Way.

"Didn't understand a thing back then," Etienne muttered. He passed the booklets back to Ciel. "Caused myself a pile of trouble."

"Uh-huh." Ciel sat forward on her seat. "What I want to know, er—is there anything really to this?"

"Made a bunch of money, though." He looked off in the distance, gnawing the licorice thoughtfully.

"That's good, of course, but did you actually *see* anything or experience anything…unusual?"

"Can't look directly into the sun, you know. Blind you for sure." The glare reflected on the lenses of his glasses and she couldn't see his eyes.

She felt incredibly foolish. "And you didn't actually, er—*ride* in a flying saucer or anything?"

"I should live so long!" he hooted, slapping his knee. "Talked to the president once, though, back in '52. No, '56? Anyway, the year Elvis went on 'Ed Sullivan'— that's how I recollect it. Strange name, Elvis. Seemed to fit, though, so that's what I called him."

"Yes, I know, but you see, about your camp—"

"Best fishing on the bayou. Guaranteed it to me."

Ciel had the feeling Etienne was drifting. She'd sabotaged her source with a blood-sugar high. "That's right, and Jack caught a whopper."

"Jack who?"

"René's friend. There're these lights and—"

With a snort, Etienne bit off the tip of his whip, then tied the rest of the strand in a bow knot and stuck it in his shirt pocket. "René, hmmph. What a stick. Just like his daddy, Melvin. That baby brother of mine still can't see the forest for the trees. Takes a special talent to notice what's right in front of your nose sometimes."

Ciel was beginning to feel a little desperate. "Yes, I understand, but what about the thumping and stuff?"

"Every man hears a different drummer, gal."

"Jack thinks it's raccoons."

Etienne made a face. "Pesky varmints. Never could stand 'em myself."

Ciel's shoulders slumped. She didn't really know what she'd been expecting, but she was surprised at the weight of her disappointment. "So it isn't angels or poltergeists or ETs—"

"Easy, you say? Hardest dern thing in the world to face, truth is."

"No, Uncle Etienne, not *easy*, ETs. You know, aliens."

He nodded sagely. "Oh, yeah. Tourists. Lots of 'em around this time of the summer, generally. Say, you got another piece of that licorice?"

Ciel sighed. "Right here."

She dug under the cushion and handed Etienne the sack again. He accepted it with as much delight as the first time, thanking her profusely. Ciel listened to his chat with half an ear, thinking hard.

So proof wasn't an easy thing to come by. Just because she'd wanted something substantial to rub Jack's nose in, to make him wake up and smell the rocket fuel, and that she hadn't gotten it from Etienne, didn't mean she had to give up.

But maybe she and Jack weren't suited. She drew a deep breath, feeling her lips heat at the mere memory of his kisses. *Yeah, right, like bacon didn't go with eggs.*

Well, it was clear that she and the rocketeer had something going on a physical level. And as upset as she'd been at his attitude after their last close encounter, after she'd had time to consider, she wasn't convinced that their differences were insurmountable. It was like space exploration, a matter of timing, careful planning and daring execution.

So, he was a workaholic on a tight schedule with his feet planted firmly on terra firma, and she was something of a daydreamer. Even though she knew Jack would have to be snatched by aliens, vivisectioned and reassembled before he'd be convinced of an extraterrestrial presence, there had to be some way to make him at least admit the *possibility* of it. Heck, the proof was all around them, if he'd only look! And if he could accept that, then there'd be a definite solar ray of hope that their relationship could work out, too. And she'd decided that she absolutely wanted something special with the spaceman.

But the only way that might happen was if she took matters into her own hands. Yes, it was time for drastic measures.

She rose and gave Etienne a kiss on the cheek. "Thanks for the visit. I'll come see you again soon."

"Bring chocolate next time."

She grinned. "You've got it. Bye."

"And Ciel?" Merry as a gnome, Etienne cast a furtive glance from side to side, gave her a broad wink and a whisper. "Elvis has left the building."

"JACK! COME QUICK! I need you." Ciel charged up the garage stairs and burst into the office.

"What?" Bleary-eyed, he jumped to his feet, nearly upsetting his computer chair. "Ciel, what now?"

"Hurry! You've got to help with my car. I'm late already. Come on!"

In a swirl of sea-foam crinkle skirts that matched her lacy tank top, she grabbed his arm and tugged him outside into the steamy afternoon. The sunshine caught the facets of her crystal pendant and reflected it back. Jack's khaki pants and striped shirt were just rumpled enough to give him a sexy appeal. She thought absently they made a good-looking couple. She almost hated to disturb him, but this was for his own good. Bullying, cajoling, she dragged him to the passenger side of her car.

"What's the trouble?" he demanded, nonplussed.

"Something's loose under the dash. Would you just get in and take a look? I'm late!"

"I'm no mechanic—"

She pulled open the door, crossed her arms belligerently and made her expression huffy. "Put you up, feed you, save you from hordes of invading tourists, and you can't do this one little bitty thing for me, Professor?"

Jaw tightening, he crawled into the passenger seat. Ciel immediately slammed the door behind him and went around to the driver's side to slide in.

Jack was bent over, inspecting the underside of her dash, his voice muffled. "I don't see anything."

"Good." She inserted the key, started the engine and headed down the drive.

Jack straightened, his features tight with suspicion. "Just what the hell do you think you're doing?"

She gave him a blithe smile. "Kidnapping you."

He gave her a startled look. "After the way I put my foot in it last time, I'm surprised you're even speaking to me."

"Let's just say you got lucky."

"This is a seduction scene from a B movie," he teased.

She rolled her eyes. "Get real. Not *that* lucky."

"Then stop the car."

"Nope."

"Ciel, I'm warning you—"

"Oh, good," she purred, "I love it when you do that."

He tried another tack. "I've got work to do."

"Your pond scum can wait."

"But—"

"This is more important, Jack."

"Now, hold on a damn minute!" He braced a hand on the dash and looked aghast as the speedometer needle soared. "My project is the whole reason I came to this deranged town in the first place."

"So you'll get back to it. But right now, you're coming with me. You're in denial, Professor, and I've got to open your eyes before it's too late!"

6

"WHAT THE HELL is that?"

Three hulking creatures in black space suits with enormous bubble heads and breathing that sounded like Darth Vader on a bad day blocked the cool elementary school corridor.

"See, I told you," Ciel said triumphantly.

"Oh." Comprehension replaced the alarm in Jack's tone. "Decontamination suits."

"Right. Would you just look at this stuff?"

She pointed to a gray-green growth climbing the cinder-block wall behind a wall-mounted water fountain. The curly, faintly powdery substance dripped from the ceiling tiles and curdled up out of the carpet.

"Good God, it's everywhere," Jack said, watching the team scrubbing and scraping at the slim.

"They can't identify it, either. Just appeared out of nowhere."

"Yeah, appeared straight out of Hollywood," he growled. "Flimflam and tinsel, not reality."

"All right, Professor. Then *you* explain it, because no one else can."

"Now *THIS* I can believe!"

"You can?"

Jack sniffed the spicy aromas pouring from the

kitchen at Benoît's Lakeside Café. "I *believe* I'll have another bowl of that gumbo—"

"Yes, sir, coming right up," the portly proprietor said.

"Another time, François," Ciel said firmly, dragging Jack around the side of the building to a row of waist-high screened bins. "Show him."

Jack groaned in disappointment. "Are you trying to torture me into capitulation?"

"Forget about your stomach, Professor. Take a close look at this."

She threw back two of the hinged tops. A scaly clattering and sinister clicking rustled out of the first, accompanied by a startlingly loud basso-profundo chorus from the second.

Curious, Jack peered inside, then recoiled. "Great Jupiter!"

François Benoît slipped on a pair of heavy-duty welder's gloves, reached one hand into each bin and withdrew two specimens.

Jack gulped and pointed a shaky finger. "Well, I've seen a lobster—"

"Lobster my sweet aunt Sadie's patootie!" Ciel cried. The five-pound brownish black crustacean Benoît brandished waved its foot-long feelers and snapped its massive claws in a frenzy. "That thing used to be a little bitty six-inch crawfish."

"Put 'em in three nights ago," François said. "Grew like Topsy, didn't it? Bullfrogs the same way."

Jack stared at the mottled, webfooted behemoth in Benoît's other hand. "Frog? I thought it was a puppy!"

"JACK, *cher*!" Marie thrust a paper plate loaded with chicken and sausage jambalaya, corn on the cob and crusty garlic bread into his hands. She had a dewy glow from the heat, and her dark eyes sparkled with welcome. "So glad you could come. Don't you just *love* family reunions?"

"Uh, haven't had much experience with them, ma'am."

She touched his shoulder in sympathy. "You poor thing. Well, we'll just fix that, won't we?"

"Yes, ma'am." Jack juggled the plate. "Thanks."

Under the metal-beamed city pavilion shed, a boom box pounded out Paul Toups and Zydecajun's rendition of "Jolie Blonde," while couples swirled, children pranced and old-timers clapped to the lively rhythm. Bowls and casseroles and boxes of food heaped the overflowing picnic tables. Lawn chairs faced the West so their owners could enjoy the last of the peach-and-marigold sunset.

"*Now* you can eat," Ciel said, and began loading her plate. "But that's not why we're here."

"I'm afraid to ask. Don't tell me if it's something disgusting that'll spoil my appetite."

Afraid she'd do it anyway, Jack hurriedly shoved a forkful of jambalaya into his mouth, then groaned in pleasure. He'd been dragged from pillar to post all afternoon by this determined redhead without so much as a sip of swamp water. Whether he'd wanted to or not, he'd seen just about every item she had listed in that notebook of hers. Videos of alleged UFOs, pop cans that didn't pop, even an octogenarian with a pistol the size of a minor satellite!

Jack chewed another bite. She'd really put some effort into it. He almost hated to tell her he still wasn't convinced.

Yes, there were some interesting phenomena at work

in Whiskey Bay, but he had no doubt that a concentrated investigation at any site in the world could produce a variety of startling and unusual wonders. And considering the Southern heat, the eccentric Southern small-town population, and the tourists' feeding frenzy out on Ballard Road, it wasn't at all remarkable that things could look a little cockeyed—especially to a ditzy female whose view of the world was already skewed.

"There he is!"

Ciel hastily set her plate down and dragged Jack across the pavilion. Desperately, he shoveled jambalaya even faster. She came up beside a portly, elderly gentleman.

"Uncle Melvin, I want you to meet Jack Cooper. Jack, Melvin Ballard, Etienne's brother and fifty years our local banker."

"Ah, René's friend." Melvin stuck out a hand. "A pleasure."

Jack balanced his plate, swallowed, shook. "Sir."

"I saw Etienne recently," Ciel said.

"I hope he wasn't...confused."

"Well, a bit."

Melvin shook his head. "Happens all too often, I'm afraid."

"I really wanted to know about those pamphlets he wrote."

The older man's look turned suddenly severe. "It was a family embarrassment. Please, we don't like to speak of it."

"But did Etienne ever talk about any unusual goings-on around his place?"

"Oh, all the time."

Ciel's eyes grew darker with excitement. "Really? What kind? Jack's had some things happen—"

"Now, wait a minute, sunshine. I never said—"

"Critters. That's all it ever was. That and Etienne's moonshine." Melvin leaned closer, conspiratorial. "Papa wanted to commit him, you know. But Mama wouldn't have it. Flying saucers, bah! This current UFO furor just proves there's a crackpot in every generation, I suppose. Nothing new under the sun."

"Oh." Ciel couldn't keep the disappointment out of her voice.

"Well, thanks for your time, sir," Jack said, pleased to have cleared up Ciel's obsession with the camp house in such a emphatic manner. Maybe she'd let the cursed thing go now. He led her away. "Satisfied, sunshine?"

"Not by a long shot, Professor." She eyed him, then sighed. "Still skeptical? I swear, you are one stubborn—"

"Ciel, darlin', come dance with me!"

She broke off at the arrival of a man with an all-American face and shoulders the size of Toledo. Something about the way he held himself suggested a proprietary interest in Ciel, and Jack felt something hot and unexpected punch him in the gut.

"Hello, Izzy." Ciel's smile was a bit uncertain. "Jack, this is Izzy Chaston. He owns the Stop and Go."

"You don't mind if I borrow her for a minute, do you, man?"

Izzy made his request with a grin that had no doubt charmed the socks—and probably other unmentionables—off of countless women.

Jack gritted his teeth. "Be my guest."

With a last helpless look over her shoulder, Izzy whisked Ciel off to the crowded dance floor. Jack couldn't help but notice the feminine eyes admiring Izzy's tight butt in tighter blue jeans, sashaying seductively to a Cajun waltz. Jack had two left feet.

Or the way those same women swooned over Izzy's brawny biceps—muscles no doubt accustomed to hoisting tons of engine steel—as they flexed against the snug, rolled-up sleeves of his chambray shirt. Jack's forte was mental muscle these days and the heaviest thing he lifted was a calculator. He grimaced.

Watching them, Jack narrowed his eyes at the way the mechanic's big hands spanned Ciel's slim waist. He felt his ears begin to heat when Izzy raised her hand to his lips and nibbled her knuckles. Something evil churned in his belly when Izzy bent and whispered in her ear, then possessively caressed her back as they danced. And worse, Ciel didn't seem to be putting up any protest.

His appetite gone, Jack tossed his unfinished dinner plate into a nearby trash can and stomped out to wait for Ciel in the car.

"What's the matter now?"

"Nothing's the matter, except I've got experiments to monitor. Thanks for dropping me off here."

Sighing, Ciel drove her Camaro up to the camp-house door. In the beam of her headlights, she could see that a few campers had pulled up stakes, leaving Jack with a modicum of privacy again. What if the tourist boom frittered out overnight? There'd be no need for him to use her office, no excuse for her even to see him again. The thought filled her with dismay.

She looked at the man seated beside her, his face shadowed by the green dashboard lights. "You're ticked that I kidnapped you, right? That I took you on a wild-goose chase, right? Well, I'm not going to apologize."

"There's no need."

"Then why are you sulking?"

He shoved his fingers through his hair in irritation. "I am not sulking!"

"Yes, you are. And it's making me cranky. That and the fact that I wasted my time trying to prove anything to a man whose mind was already made up."

"Look, just because I don't want to play Buck Rogers doesn't mean I haven't found the day, er—interesting."

"Then you'll admit that something really strange is happening in Whiskey Bay?" Delighted, she turned to him eagerly, threw her arms around his neck and kissed his cheek. "Wonderful! I need the scientist in you to help me figure things out, Jack. We've got so much to investigate, but there has to be a common thread. This could be the story of the century and—"

"Whoa, there." Stiffening, he held her away by the shoulders, shifting uncomfortably on the car seat. "I never said anything like that."

"Oh." She slumped, and her mouth trembled. "My mistake."

"Ciel, don't." He bent closer, brushed his lips over hers. Then pulled back abruptly when her mouth softened. His voice was strangled. "This isn't a good idea."

"Why not?"

"In a word, Izzy."

"Izzy is old news."

"Maybe he shouldn't be."

"What do you mean?"

He turned back to her in exasperation. "Good-looking man, owns his own business, and he dotes on you. Probably as close to a perfect husband as you're likely to find in Whiskey Bay. You'd be a fool not to snap up a hot prospect like that."

"What if I don't want him?"

"Then what, Ciel?" His voice was rough, and he latched his hand around her nape, dragging her up against his chest so that her crystal pendant poked them both. Bending his head, he kissed her hard, almost as if he were punishing her—or himself. "Is this what you want?"

His sudden loss of control excited her. Here was the passionate, feeling individual she knew lived beneath his calm façade. Trembling, she stared up at him, her answer the barest whisper of sound. "Yes."

"Damn you, that's not good enough."

Bewildered, she gasped. "I don't understand."

"Do you know what seeing Izzy with you did to me?" he growled, his angry breath fanning her cheeks. "Made me jealous as hell, that's what. I can't do a damn thing to control it!"

Her tremulous sigh contained an element of helpless laughter. "You scientific types always make everything so complicated."

"I want you, sunshine—you know that. But someone like Izzy can offer you a lot more than I can. I'm not good at relationships. I'm not good for you."

She stroked his lean cheek, loving the rasp of his beard against her fingertips. "Let me be the judge of that."

Jack narrowed his eyes, and gave her a little shake. "Listen to me, Ciel. I learned the hard way the first time around. Retha said I just couldn't give enough, and then she left. I won't risk it again."

Ciel heard the self-condemnation and the fear in his voice. No wonder he didn't want to open himself up to that kind of hurt again, and yet by cutting himself off from the joys of love and intimacy, how much of life he'd be missing!

But would he ever be able to see that? She knew that under his reserve there beat the heart of a sensitive, caring man. All he needed was someone to bring out his best qualities, someone he could trust who'd never let him down as Retha had. Ciel knew that whatever the risks to her heart, she had to try.

She pressed her mouth against his, murmuring encouragement. "You're selling yourself short. I won't let that happen again."

He groaned, tightening his arms around her, then taking her hand and placing it over the hardness straining the front of his pants. "You see what you do to me? I know we'll be good together physically, but that's all I can offer."

"It's enough."

For now, her heart whispered. Desire was a start. And she knew that he cared about her in many ways already. With her care, he'd come to trust her and give himself up to the ardor she knew he was capable of.

His tone was strangled. "Ciel, I'm trying to be honest with you, but you're not making it easy."

"Don't you know me at all yet, Jack? I always go against type." Laughing softly, she pulled his head down to hers.

They nearly didn't make it inside. Somehow, as they crossed the porch into the camp house, Jack was kissing her and she lost her sandals. Her hands were under his shirt, and she and Jack fell over the threshold tangled in a heated embrace. Jack slammed the door behind them, then pressed her back against the wooden panels, skimming his palm up her thigh, bunching the gauzy skirt around her hips and grinding himself against her.

"Oh, my," she breathed, ignited by the power of his need.

"If you're having second thoughts, tell me now."

"This Daring Blonde? Never." Grasping his head in her hands, she pulled his face to hers, nipping at his lips, laving the underside of his jaw with her tongue, tasting the salt of his skin and his unique male essence.

When he couldn't stand her teasing any longer, he groaned and took her mouth again, plunging his tongue deeply, exploring the sweetness of her response, until she was hardly able to stand but for his support. Fretfully, she tugged at his shirt, and he whipped it over his head. In the darkness he was strong and mysterious and powerfully male, and she touched him reverently, letting her hands slide up the corded muscles of his rib cage, then circle his flat, bronze nipples. He shuddered uncontrollably, and she smiled and touched her tongue there, just so.

He went rigid, his fingers digging into her curls. "Ah, sunshine, what you do to me."

"What we do to each other. It's heavenly."

"Out of this world."

With another lingering kiss, he cupped her breasts through the thin tank top, then moved to her waist, shoving the elasticized band of her skirt down over her hips to the floor, leaving her in shirt and silky bikini panties. Holding her hips, he knelt and nuzzled her abdomen, evoking a gasp of pleasure as his tongue found the indentation of her navel.

She swayed drunkenly, awash with sensation, then his warm breath found her most secret folds through the thin silk and she cried out. His fingers tightened on her buttocks, sliding beneath the elastic trim of her undergarment, gently squeezing and tormenting her flesh.

"Easy, sunshine. Don't you like it?"

"Too much," she admitted on a hoarse whisper, her fingers twisting in his hair. She felt as if she were dissolving into a cascade of exquisite sensation and she had to hold on, or plummet off the end of the world. He held her prisoner while he worked his wiles, until she was writhing, nearly sobbing with pleasure. "Jack, please..."

Rising, he scooped her into his strong arms, holding her against his chest and striding unerringly through the darkened house to the sparsely furnished bedroom. Starshine fell through the windows, reflected off the water behind the camp. He didn't bother with the lamp, but lowered her to the soft bedspread, then shucked his shoes and pants and lay beside her.

She reached for him eagerly, running her hands over his powerful shoulders, tracing the bulge of his biceps. Catching the hem of her shirt, he tugged it over her head and then removed her bra, freeing her breasts to the feverish explorations of his fingers. Her crystal pendant lay cool and satiny against her heated skin. Ciel gulped as he plucked at her nipples, gently scoring their pebbled tips until they were hard and aching. When he bent his head and took one into his mouth, she sighed on a high note of pleasure, feeling the tug of his lips all the way to the simmering center of her being.

He feasted on her, savoring the textures and nuances, murmuring praise and husky love words, melting her with his voice, with his touch. And she returned the favors, stroking the cords in his strong neck, sliding her fingers under the band of his briefs to explore the hollows of his lean hips, tantalizing him with the touch of her tongue to his earlobe. When he shuddered with pleasure, his whole body tensile and struggling with the effort to pace their joining, she exulted, empowered by the instinctive feminine knowledge that his response, his need, was for her alone. It made her bold.

Sliding her hands forward along his hipbones, she

touched him intimately, exploring his hardness. He jerked and groaned, crushing her to him, finding her mouth again, sending her reeling with the power of his kiss. His weight was a welcome pressure, and everywhere their skin touched, Ciel felt the heat of a thousand suns.

"Ah, sunshine, I don't think I can wait..."

She laughed softly, relishing his admission, confessing her own. "Neither can I."

It was all he needed. With eager hands, he removed her panties and kicked off his briefs, then reached into a bedside drawer for protection. Tenderly, Jack gathered Ciel close.

In the star-struck dimness, they smiled at each other, wondering at their unique rapport, the ease and trust that flowed and linked them at this instant. Even though the hunger rode them equally, they paused, taking the time to set the moment in their memories, subtly building the anticipation, letting the rush of blood and thud of hearts ignite their fever to the heights they both knew awaited them.

Jack touched her temple, threading his fingers through her vibrant curls. "Ciel..."

Shifting her weight, she showed him her acceptance, her eagerness for him. "Yes."

Gently, he opened her thighs and positioned himself, probing her wet, silky depths. Bending her knees, Ciel gasped at the exquisite fullness, catching his hips to pull him closer, faster. With a groaned curse, Jack thrust fully, claiming her completely.

Ciel clung to him, gasping and lost to the power of this joining. Arching, unable to get close enough, she rose to meet him as he began to move. She touched her lips to the place over his heart, feeling the thunder rocketing under his skin, and he went wild. Capturing her mouth, he kissed her forcefully, until silver spangles danced behind her eyelids, all the while taking her with his body to a place she'd never imagined existed.

When they plunged together into fulfillment, Ciel's soft cry of ecstasy triggered Jack's release. Shuddering, trembling, they held on to each other, pleasured, united, rejoicing.

IT WAS that funny light that appears just before dawn that woke her. Or maybe it was the soft, rhythmic rattle of something in the rafters. Perhaps it was simply the presence she sensed standing at the window.

Smiling, Ciel lay quietly on her side, naked and satiated under the thin sheet, watching Jack. Nude, his back to her, he braced himself against the window facing, awaiting the sun. He was magnificent, lean with a runner's musculature. She loved looking at him, found pleasure in watching him unawares. She lay very still, keeping her breathing even, to enjoy the richness of such luxury.

Tenderness consumed her, mingled with an equal amount of exasperation. No man could have taken such care with a woman as he had unless he felt for her something deep and emotionally connecting. Yet his stubborn refusal even to acknowledge Ciel's concerns about the phenomena affecting Whiskey Bay was seriously puzzling.

Was he simply so closed to new, perhaps radical, ideas? Or so terrified of this intimate connection with her he dared not risk even the remotest hint of empathy with her agenda? She couldn't believe such cowardice of him. It was almost as if he were covering something up....

Ciel frowned, her eyes tracing the tense line of Jack's spine. What if those television reporters had been onto something? Could Jack really have been sent by NASA to secretly investigate the UFO site after all? If that was true, it would make perfect sense for him to deny any interest in the occurrence in order to keep a low profile and compile his findings without interference. Especially interference from a nosy reporter!

That had to be it. Furious at her own stupidity at being too dense to figure this out before, she opened her mouth to demand he tell her the truth, then froze.

At the window, shaggy head bent, arms braced, Jack stood as beautiful and still as a Michelangelo statue—a living, breathing statue who was suddenly, inexplicably, bathed in an eerie, blue-green bath of light.

Ciel couldn't breathe, couldn't blink, but then there was a flurry of sound, like a distant drumroll, and she did blink and the light was gone. As she lay there paralyzed, her heart rammed against her breastbone like a wild bird.

And then Jack moved, turning to pull on a pair of ragged cutoffs, moving quietly so as not to awaken her, everything normal again in the pale predawn light so that she could have imagined it. But she knew she hadn't.

Quivering beneath her skin, Ciel slammed her eyes shut, forcing herself to breathe evenly when she knew he stood over her, watching her. Then the soft slap of his bare soles against the tiles, then the creak of the back door, then nothing.

With a gasp, Ciel scrambled up against the headboard, her trembling fingers pressed to her lips. What was the source of that light? Or who...?

7

HOOK, LINE AND SINKER.

A misty light drifted through the moss-hung oaks and flickered like buccaneer's silver on the mottled surface of the bayou. Jack cast his fishing line, and the shiny metal lure arched through the thick air, landing with a tiny splash at the knobby base of a water cypress. With proper care, the bass he was after would take the bait, and then he'd be a goner.

Poor old fish. Jack knew just how it felt.

When had it happened? When Ciel had first looked at him with those guileless blue eyes that so quickly turned mischievous? When he'd stolen his first taste of her luscious mouth? Or when he'd risen this morning after a night of her generous and honest passion and seen the tumble of whiskey-colored curls on his pillow and the angel innocence in her sleeping countenance?

Jack stifled a groan of dismay. This wasn't in his game plan by any means. Damn it to hell, he didn't need emotional complications in his life! He'd made it clear to Ciel. Hadn't he been listening to his own spiel?

The vibration of footfalls on the wooden dock caught his attention and he turned and stared. No makeup, hair a curling mass of ringlets, all slim, freckled legs and bare feet under the swirl of her green skirts, Ciel walked hesitantly toward him, her expression uncertain, her fingers worrying her crystal pendant like some kind of talisman.

In fact, he thought with alarm, she was almost as green as her tank top.

"Is something wrong?" He dropped the fishing rod by his open tackle box, wiped his hands on a frayed handkerchief, then reached for her elbow.

"Wrong?" She jumped at his touch, and her cheeks paled. Sliding from beneath his grasp, she pasted on a bright smile. "No, why do you ask?"

He frowned, peering at her. Her gaze skittered nervously from his. Jack knew he wasn't the Master of Morning Afters, but good God, could he have been that bad in bed? "You look a little sick."

Ciel caught a startled breath. "I—I don't do mornings very well, and I've got to get to work if I expect to get a paper out this week."

Second thoughts? That she appeared to be in the throes of a bad case of them just as he was pricked Jack's ego in a curious fashion. What was she thinking? Sure, they'd enjoyed something rare, but they weren't on the same wavelength and they both knew it. Maybe *she* was trying to let *him* down easy. But allowing her to do it was easier said than done, he found.

"Yeah, I've got work to do, too, but to hell with it."

Hauling her to him, he pulled her into the vee of his legs and took her mouth. Ciel gasped and stiffened, but he continued to kiss her until she softened against his bare chest. He felt himself falling into a vortex of feeling from which there could be no recovery.

Her hands moved upward, curving about his neck, exploring, pressing the muscles, probing. Abandoning his neck, she swept fingers into his hair, massaging his skull all over, lingering at the back of his head. He released her lips.

"Ouch. Take it easy, sunshine."

She jerked out of his embrace, hiding her hands guiltily behind her and taking a step back. "Sorry."

"Jeez, Ciel, relax."

"Oh." She stared at him, sapphire eyes so glazed they nearly crossed, and gave a tiny shudder.

"My God, you are sick!" Jack stepped closer, noticing the haze of perspiration dewing her upper lip.

"I'm fine. Really. Are you catching anything?"

"Nary a nibble." Consternated by her distraction, he scowled. "Watch out—you'll get stabbed. Those hooks are sharp."

She turned to him, holding out a colorful lure in the middle of the old handkerchief. "Oh, look, a mollie bait. Haven't seen one like this in a while. What's this thingie called, Jack?"

"What, this?" He shrugged and poked at the lure with his index finger. "It's a swivel—ouch! Damn it!"

He stared at his bloody fingertip in amazement. If he hadn't known better, he'd have sworn Ciel had deliberately impaled him on that hook!

"Oh, Jack, I'm so sorry!"

She was full of contrition, and her freckles stood out against the abnormal milkiness of her skin.

"Here, let me help."

She blotted the wound with the kerchief, spotting the cloth with crimson, making appropriate soothing noises until the tiny puncture quit oozing. Shoving the handkerchief into her pocket, she gave Jack a tremulous smile. "All better?"

"You're really wired, aren't you?"

"Oh, no, I'm fine," she protested again. "But I've got to go—"

He shoved his abused hand through his hair in exasperation. "Listen, sunshine, I don't know where this is going, either, so if you need some time, okay."

"No, it's not that," Ciel said in a quaking voice.

"Well, that's a relief." Confused, he stared at her. "I swear sometimes I can't figure you out at all!"

Despite the sultriness of the morning air, her teeth were actually chattering. Brushing her hair back, she gave him a brave smile. "That's good—I mean, keeping the mystery alive in a relationship is very important, don't you think?"

"Well, you're the one who's been asking all the questions, but I think you'll find there's always a logical answer—" He broke off, wrinkling his nose. "Something's fishy here."

She backed down the dock, laughing shrilly.

"Oh, no, Jack. I've never met a man—" the shrillness changed to something strangled "—with such a suspicious nature. You really ought to work on that...."

"I'll take it under advisement. But what I meant was, don't you smell something? Look!"

He pointed at the water. Silver scales glinting, no less than a hundred hand-sized perch, bass and crappie floated belly-up on the sluggish current beneath the dock, all bloated with death.

"My gosh!" Ciel gasped. "Did you do that?"

"Me? All I've done is dip a hook." Jack stared at the carcasses and shook his head. "All right, Ciel. I guess I'll have to admit the truth."

"Oh, no. I don't want to know anything," she wheezed. "Truly I don't."

"Well, here it is anyway, sunshine. I admit I've been fighting this like hell, but you're onto something."

"I am?" She licked her upper lip and looked faintly queasy. "Just my luck."

"You've been trying to convince me all along you know what's going on around here. So here's your chance to prove it. Come on."

He grabbed her hand and tugged her toward the shore.

"Come on where?" she asked, dragging her feet.

"Back to the landing site."

"WHAT DO YOU MEAN we can't take a look?" Jack demanded.

"Mayor's orders."

Jack gave Deputy Cleveland Henderson a frustrated glare that included the yards and yards of yellow-and-black crime-scene tape barricading the approach to the rice field landing site. Despite this unexpected obstruction to Whiskey Bay's leading tourist attraction, a steady stream of cars and pedestrians still moved up and down Ballard Road. The rich aromas of frying funnel cakes and chicory-laced coffee filled the air, and crafts vendors hawked their wares in the morning heat.

"Deputy, it's imperative I take another look at that rice field. Ciel, tell him who I am."

"Dr. Cooper is a highly respected NASA exobiologist."

"Sorry." Cleveland crossed his brawny arms across his khaki-covered chest, his dark face creased with regret. "I got my orders."

"Thus roasting the goose that lays the golden tourist dollar eggs around here," Ciel mused.

"It's interfering with the conduct of legitimate business."

"Sonny Prejean complaining again, I guess." She turned to Jack with a hopeful look. "Well, Jack, too bad. I guess we'll have to pass."

"Not if I can help it," he muttered. "Kyle has a boat, right?"

"Ah, yes."

"Let's go."

Grabbing her arm, he propelled her back the way they'd come, thinking hard.

But Ciel suddenly dug in her sandals. "Hold it a minute. I forgot to tell Cleveland something for Mama."

"Okay. Hurry it up," he growled.

Ciel darted back to the deputy, pulled him down to whisper in his ear and passed him something from her pocket. Then she returned to Jack's side, steps faltering.

He raised an eyebrow. "What was that all about?"

"Nothing. Nothing at all."

Despite her bright answer, she looked guilty. Jack wondered what she was plotting now. And her color still didn't look so good. Grabbing his wallet, he went to a booth and bought a fried funnel cake and two coffees.

"Eat," he said, thrusting the sugary pastry at her.

"I'm not hungry."

"Look, if the Blob can devour an entire town, you can manage to swallow a little doughnut."

"You're right. I should try to keep my strength up." She pinched off a piece and took a tentative bite.

"Atta girl."

WHY HAD JACK suddenly made an about-face in his attitude toward her investigations? Something wasn't right.

Seated at the tiller of the dented metal bateau attached to an ancient Evinrude motor, Ciel touched her crystal for reassurance—not that Aunt Tee-Ta's charm had done her a bit of good—and edged the craft up the meandering moss-draped bayou through the tunnel of overgrown oaks and cypresses. In the bow, Jack kept up a perfect imitation of the Dull Professor, gathering soil, plant and water samples into bottles and zipper bags.

Under his direction, they'd spent the day following the bayou around to the back of the rice field landing site to collect samples and then backtracking the evidence of the fish kill up the sluggish waterway.

He bottled up yet another water sample and happily scribbled on the label. "I can run a few simple diagnostic tests tonight, and if anything turns up shoot them off to the lab first thing—"

Right, she thought. But what was the true purpose for this expedition? And how could she get him to let her go without arousing his suspicions?

"There!" Jack pointed to a tributary curling off the primary waterway. A stinky pile of pewter-colored fish floated in the reeds. "This way."

Ciel bit her lip. They'd gone far enough. "I'm not sure where this ends up, Jack."

"Don't worry, sunshine, I'm a whiz at navigation."

Ciel had no choice but to guide the boat where Jack indicated through the circuitous channel. The thick, overhanging vegetation cut off the light and made the water as black as octopus ink. The musty smell of decay clotted the thick air. The waterway branched off in several places, the land on either side turning swampy, and Ciel couldn't see the main channel anymore.

The sense of disorientation made her increasingly nervous. "It's getting late. Don't you think we ought to turn back?"

Jack inspected the thickening twilight with satisfaction. "We're on schedule."

A shiver scampered down her back. Whose schedule? For what? It was time to stop being such a wimp. What would Sylvie Fairstar do in her position? Brazen it out, that's what. "Well, I've had enough. I want to go home. *Now.*"

"Cool your jets. All you had to do was say so."

The steam went out of her. She increased the engine throttle, then looked around, hesitated. "Uh, Jack? Which way?"

Scanning the swampy landscape on either side, he pointed with authority. "There."

Thirty minutes later, Ciel peered anxiously through the near blackness while the outboard motor coughed and spluttered. "Are we nearly there? We're running low on gas."

"Great."

"Don't blame me," she protested, instantly defensive, then choked on her words. *Great?* What did he mean by that? Had he planned on stranding them all along? Had he been leading her on a wild-goose chase the whole time? What was going on?

"Look, I've really got to get back," she said, desperation making her voice go high. "I didn't realize I'd signed on for an excursion down the Amazon."

Jack was a shadowy form in the front of the boat, nearly indistinguishable from the overhanging tree limbs he tried to push out of their way. His voice was a calm, disembodied vibration, echoing hollowly under the canopy of vegetation. "Actually, this looks more like the Orinoco."

"I don't care if it's Disneyland! I've had enough of you and the wilderness, and we're going back if we have to paddle the whole way, so—"

"Won't do any good."

She spluttered. "Why not?"

"We're lost."

"No, no, no." She shook her head in disbelief just as the engine gave a final cough and died. Releasing the tiller, she braced her hands on the side of the gently swaying boat and fought seasickness. "How can a man who's made six hundred earth orbits be *lost?*"

"It happens."

"You planned this all along," she accused shakily.

Jack watched her over his shoulder, his eyes glinting with an otherworldly light. "Oh, absolutely. Turnabout is fair play, you see. I'm kidnapping *you* this time."

"I'M TELLING YOU, that wasn't quicksand."

"Yeah, you said something about knowing how to navigate, too."

Grimacing at Ciel's jittery tone, Jack adjusted another palmetto branch over the framework of a lean-to he was constructing under a stunted water oak. Irritation, impatience and chagrin clipped his words short. "Just hold that flashlight steady, will you?"

Except for the small circle of illumination, the swamp was pitch-black; dark, ominous shapes loomed against even darker gloom. A symphony of night sounds reverberated under the canopy of lush vegetation—bullfrogs; crickets; the sibilant trickle of water; the distant, eerie scream of some predator. Even though some of the day's heat had dissipated with the setting sun, the humidity made the air as thick as buttermilk. Out of gas, they'd had no option but to tie up the boat and seek out a likely spot well back from the edge of the bayou to spend the night.

"Good thing Kyle's a Boy Scout, huh?" Ciel asked. "At least *someone* came prepared."

"Yeah, peachy. I'm really looking forward to a meal of Vienna sausages and oatmeal cream cookies." Jack unfolded a purple plastic rain poncho emblazoned with an LSU Tigers logo, which they'd found in the boat with Kyle's stash of supplies, and spread it on the grassy floor of the lean-to.

She looked dubiously at the poncho. "Think that will ward off the water moccasins?"

"Ciel!"

"Then there are the 'gators—"

"There aren't any alligators around here."

"Bubba Cantrell caught one twenty-two and a half feet long right out of this very bayou. Made the prettiest pair of custom boots you ever saw. Good thing, too, 'cause of Bubba's losing those three toes when he tried to pull the critter into his boat—"

"So don't wander off, okay? What's the matter with you?"

Jack shoved his hands through his hair. "Look, this babbling isn't helping."

"Sorry." What was wrong with her? Cool it. Or else apologizing was going to become a habit.

Jack inspected her features, stiff and strained in the flashlight's yellow beam. She glanced at him, then shot a look toward the heavens. Jeez, she was really spooked. It was clear jungle roughing it wasn't her cup of tea. That was disappointing, too, because he'd been sure she had a secret adventurous streak. He'd even begun to picture them together camped in the Brazilian rain forest.

Hold your countdown, space jockey! Where had that thought come from? A long-term relationship with this fey creature? Was he nuts? She'd drive him mad within a week. If he didn't kill himself making love to her nonstop.

The way he wanted to do at this very moment.

But another look at her pale face made him sigh and decide that was out of the question. What she needed was reassurance, not some horny professor trying to take advantage of her.

He smoothed a hand over the curve of her bare shoulder, felt her jump and frowned. "Try to take it easy, sunshine. We'll sit tight tonight and find our way out of here at first light. It may not be as comfortable as the Holiday Inn, but everything's going to be all right."

"Oh, yeah. Sure." She raised her eyes again, peering through the leafy canopy toward the starlit sky, almost as if she were waiting for something.

"I'm not going to let anything happen to you, Ciel. You—you're too important to me. To everybody in Whiskey Bay. To the whole universe."

He tried to offer comfort again, sliding his arm around her shoulders. The light she held bobbled uncontrollably, and she stiffened against him, cutting him to the quick. He lost his temper.

"Look, we're never going to get through this—"

Jack broke off. The horror in her expressive face told it all. With all the weird Whiskey Bay occurrences, then the second thoughts following their lovemaking, now this lost-in-the-Amazon Indiana Jones adventure, she'd worked herself into a hysterical frenzy.

There was one surefire way to take her mind off the situation. He took her mouth, controlling her gasp of surprise with the powerful staking of his claim. She froze, shivered, then slid her arms around his neck, all tension melting from her. Jack deepened the kiss, stroking the inside of her mouth, finding it all spice and honey and seduction. He reveled in the way she met his invasion, with a primitive, earthy enjoyment and need that sent him soaring to the flashpoint in the flicker of an eyelash.

Alone in the wilderness, they were as new as Adam

and Eve, their hunger as old as eternity. He felt as though there had never been another woman before this one, that he was the first man to claim her. Wildfire surged through Jack's veins, and his body grew hard. He had to have her. Now.

Covering her body with his, he pressed his knee between her thighs, using the friction generated there to build the wildness between them. She whimpered into his mouth, a searching, yearning sound. He removed her shirt and unclasped her bra, cupping her breasts. Ciel arched upward, hanging on to his neck, rubbing the ball of her foot down the back of his jeans-clad calf.

Releasing her mouth, he bent his head, licking her distended nipples, using the rasp of his tongue so that they pebbled into hard buds. She tasted of salt and sweet woman's flesh, and she keened a high note when he took one pouty tip deep in his mouth and suckled strongly. She thrashed beneath him, wild with need.

Groping for his jeans snap, she opened the placket, stroking his hardness with fervent fingertips, urging him onward to madness.

He'd never felt such desire, such tender compulsion. She made him crazy with her off-the-wall lunacy, crazier still with her fiery passion. Every emotional bastion, every defense, crumbled at the mere knowledge that she existed, that she shared her uniqueness with him. And he could never get enough.

He knew that his kisses were bruising, but she welcomed them, returned them with power of her own. Something vibrated in his throat, something he couldn't contain, the primal sound of a male claiming his mate. Pushing aside her skirts and undergarments, he rolled onto his back and pulled her astride him.

Cocooned in the darkness, directed by touch and an

unerring instinct, Jack clenched his fingers on Ciel's hips, letting her guide their passion. Her disheveled half nudity was an erotic counterpoint to his fully clothed state, the satiny skin of her bare legs and hips against soft denim a tactile stimulant that nearly sent him over the edge. She balanced her hands on his shoulders, then settled over his erection. Liquid and ready and on fire, she caught her breath as the sweet pull of gravity joined them and he filled her completely.

Jack had never felt anything so good, so right, and he touched her breasts and groaned. "Sunshine..."

"Oh, yes." Ciel melted across his chest, her arms around his neck, her lips soft, warm, incredibly giving.

Pressing his palms into the small of her back, he held her tight, moving in a rhythm as old as life itself, building the night music to a tumultuous crescendo. Moisture popped out on his skin; his brain fogged; his body strained toward the ultimate release. Thrusting upward, he swirled himself against her. A cry broke from her throat, and her back arched, the inner contractions overtaking her unexpectedly, pushing her into a shuddering completion that made him smile into the night with male pride and satisfaction at what he could bring his woman.

By damn, she couldn't doubt who he was *now*.

And then she moved over him and he was lost, pitched headfirst into a thunderous release that went on and on, giving her everything he had, taking everything she could give and exulting in the life-affirming exchange.

After a long while, when their breathing slowed, he kissed her ear, her neck, the hollow where her crystal pendant lay, and whispered, "Satisfied?"

She gave him a coquettish smile. "Mmm, no...."

"You want more...?" He stroked her back.

"Rocket man, I was hoping you'd offer."

8

"EVERYONE GETS LOST. Even NASA rocket men."

"Don't start that again." Jack was a silhouette illuminated by a foggy dawn that made the swamp as surreal as a Dali painting. "I thought we got all that straight last night."

Ciel picked her way to where he was standing behind the lean-to, her smile sheepish, rueful, teasing. "Actually, I'm just teasing."

He snorted. "Figures."

"Sure you don't want one of Kyle's oatmeal pies?"

"No, thanks, I—oh, hell! Would you look at that?"

The disgust in Jack's voice startled Ciel. She followed the direction of his gaze, then stifled a gasp of surprise.

Not fifty yards away loomed a tall chain-link fence. Metal Keep Out signs emblazoned with the Prejean Oil and Engineering logo hung at intervals. Ghostly shapes of buildings and tractor-trailer rigs and stacks of oil drums drifted in and out of sight behind curling wisps of fog.

"If I'd only explored a little farther," Jack said, "we could have avoided an uncomfortable night."

"I didn't hear any complaints, Professor." Ciel leaned against him, brushing her lips to his.

Jack's fingers tightened momentarily on her shoulders, then dropped away. "Certainly scared the bejesus out of me. Come on, time for E.T. to phone home."

They fought their way through the thick foliage around the perimeter of the fence, looking for an entrance, crossing a drainage ditch that dipped beneath the chain-link fencing. Even with Jack's help, the span was nearly too wide for Ciel, and she stumbled, gave a little whoop of dismay—and ended up with both feet sinking into six inches of slimy, evil-smelling mud.

"Eech!" Levering herself from the ooze, she wrinkled her nose, daring Jack to release the grin that quivered on his lips. "The slime in this place could sprout all sorts of malignant, mankind-eating monsters."

"You've got to cut back on the sci-fi, sunshine," he informed her solemnly, watching as she squatted to rinse each shoe in the sluggish water and then put it back on. "I believe this compulsive psychosis can be successfully treated with shock therapy—"

"That's strange," she interrupted, pointing down the stream. "See where all that grass and vines and stuff is wilted down? Looks like a half-moon, doesn't it? Ohmigosh! It's half of a perfect circle!"

"So?" Puzzled, he stepped to the edge of the drooping vegetation and dropped to his haunches to examine it.

"Don't you understand?" Excited, she moved beside him, clenching his shirt in her eagerness. "Jack, this looks just like the rice field did that first day—it's another landing site!"

"And where did you get your degree—Starfleet Academy? You're getting carried away again...."

"I'm telling you it's the same thing!" she shouted. "Don't you believe me?"

He rose to his feet, the expression in his eyes pained. "It not a question of believing you. But it's a little premature to say this was caused by a spaceship! That's what started all the uproar in Whiskey Bay in the first place.''

"Listen, you—yesterday you were all for figuring out what's going on. Here's your chance to solve the mystery.''

"I'd wager this is more likely to be related to the fish kill than to alien invaders.''

"So prove it," she challenged. "You admitted it yourself—*something* is going on around here!''

The muscle in Jack's jaw grew taut. "We'll take some samples, okay? Will that satisfy you?''

"You're the boss. But after coming this far, I say we shouldn't give up without a complete investigation.''

He cast a glance back at the fence. "Inside.''

"It's a logical step.''

"Don't play Mr. Spock again with me, sunshine!'' Jack pointed his index finger at her nose. "Logic is not where you're coming from.''

"So call it a gut feeling. You know it's worth a look around. Are you game or not?''

Mouth a flat line, he cursed under his breath and she knew she'd won. "Oh, *hell.* Come on.''

After a scratchy navigation through the thorny undergrowth, they eventually came to the drive leading into the Prejean Oil work yards. Although it was still early and the dusty hard-packed industrial grounds appeared deserted except for a diesel truck idling in front of a drab prefab metal office building, the double chain-link main gates stood wide open. Anticipation and nervousness churned Ciel's insides. Eyes darting, she practically danced through the gate, tugging Jack reluctantly up the gravel road.

"I feel like *James Bond Meets the Three Stooges,*'' he grumbled.

"We've been stranded all night, right? We're telling the truth when we say we're looking for a phone—" She came up short, then jerked him in a new direction. "This way!"

Crouching in a run, Ciel ducked behind a towering stack of blue-painted oil drums, then led Jack past rows of wooden pallets loaded with more drums and oil field equipment of every description—chains, pipes, steel rods, grappling hooks, couplers.

"I think the drainage ditch is over here," she said, peeking around the corner of a pallet piled eight feet high with wooden crates marked "Surplus." Then she realized she was talking to herself. Glancing back, she found Jack bent over a basketball-sized ant mound heaped against the base of another pallet. "What's the matter? Jack, over here!"

"Interesting morphology." He stirred the mound with the toe of his shoe, frowning. "Little if any activity. Could be correlated to—"

Ciel hissed at him, gesturing. "Save it for later! Come on."

Rolling his eyes, Jack joined her at the base of the pallet. "Is all this clandestine stuff strictly necessary?"

"I don't know. What do you think?" She pointed around the corner.

Jack took a look, then let out a low whistle. Hidden behind this wall of crates, another fence faced them, six feet high and fashioned of chain link threaded with plastic ribbon to make an impenetrable visual blockade. The gate sported double padlocks and a sign bearing a skull and crossbones and the word "Danger" inside a lightning bolt.

"Must be a reason they don't want anybody in there," she said.

Jack's voice was dry. "Yeah, like Dobermans, maybe?"

"They'd be barking by now," she said dismissively.

"What about high voltage? Poisonous reptiles? Sinkholes?"

Ciel's blue eyes sparkled. "So we'll be careful. Give me a boost over?"

"Ciel, wait!"

But she'd already dashed to the gate, stuck her toe into a space and begun scaling the chain link. Cursing her impulsiveness, Jack followed, steadying her with a hand on her rounded bottom.

"What do you see?" he grunted, trying to help her balance as the wire gate swayed back and forth like a palm tree in a typhoon.

"Nothing yet." Panting, she struggled for better purchase so she could swing her leg over the top. "If I can just—"

"Hold it right there, you two!"

Ciel froze, staring over her shoulder in horror. Two burly security guards in blue uniforms pointed ugly-looking revolvers at them. Sonny Prejean stood between the guards, glaring at the intruders. Bull-chested in a pearl-studded Western shirt, his black eyes mere slits in his corpulent face, he sported cowboy boots with three-inch heels to make up for his small Cajun stature.

"What the hell do you think you're doing?" His voice was a high-pitched whine of fury.

Jack groaned. "Just what I was asking myself."

Ciel was suddenly very conscious that Jack's hand still supported a very private portion of her anatomy. She gulped, her cheeks bright pink, but she was hoping to brazen it out even from atop her incriminating six-foot perch.

"Oh, hello." She gave a weak smile. "Actually, Mr. Prejean, we're lost."

"Lost my ass!" He stalked forward, his skinny legs encased in starched blue jeans; he looked for all the world like an apple on toothpicks. "And I'm Elvis!"

"Ciel, come down," Jack instructed. Reaching for her, he spoke to Prejean over his shoulder. "Tell your men to put those guns away. Our boat ran out of gas—"

"Trespassers!" Prejean shrieked. "I tell you I'm sick to death of 'em and—wait a minute! You're that newspaper gal, ain't ya?"

Ciel jumped the last three feet to the ground, then beamed at Prejean. "That's right. You see, Dr. Cooper and I—"

Sonny Prejean jabbed a stubby finger at her. "You're the one! Dad-blame it, starting all this mess with little green men, tourists everywhere, nosing around, disrupting life, stealing souvenirs, causing all sorts of havoc so's a man can't even do an honest day's work anymore!"

Ciel blinked at Prejean's vehemence. "Well, I wouldn't say that exactly..."

"Well, I would, missy, and I've had it up to here!" Sonny Prejean made a chopping motion across his Adam's apple and glared at her. "And just so's you know I mean business, I'm going to make an example of you and your accomplice!"

"It's just about the tackiest thing I ever heard of," Lauren Herbert said indignantly. "Why, that fingerprint ink just *ruined* your manicure!"

Ciel shot her petite assistant an impatient look through the bars of the Whiskey Bay Sheriff's Annex holding cell. "Just sign the papers and bail us out of here, Lauren!"

In their sweaty, disheveled, frustrated states, she and Jack looked like hurricane refugees, but that was the least of her worries. Jack sat on the edge of a wobbly cot behind Ciel in the attitude of Rodin's *The Thinker*. He hadn't moved so much as a hair since they'd been booked for trespassing, breaking and entering and a wide assortment of other misdemeanors.

He was ominously quiet.

He was making Ciel extremely nervous.

"All right," Lauren said, snapping her chewing gum, "keep your wig on. Cleveland's processing the paperwork now." The deputy in question sat at a nearby desk, pecking with two fingers at an old Underwood typewriter. Lauren arched an eyebrow at Ciel mischievously. "Think old man Crenshaw will consider bail a legitimate business expense?"

"He'd better, since it was incurred in pursuit of a story for his newspaper."

"Well, I have to take back everything I said about his being a skinflint. I tell you, when he sent over that new computer system yesterday, I could have swallowed my gum, and almost did." Lauren's dark eyes sparkled. "It's a beaut! I've already got all the news and half the ad copy set for this week. What do you think about 'Final Frontier Days' for this week's merchants' promotion?"

"Catchy." Ciel mentally reviewed her "to do" list for getting out another edition of the *Press*. "And I'll put together some copy for you about our arrests as soon as they let us out of here. Hey, did you think to bring a camera? A picture of us behind bars would look great on the front page."

"The hell you say!" Jack surged to his feet. The first move he'd made in an hour caused Ciel to jump backward against the steel bars. The ferocious scowl on his face made her sorry they were both on the same side of those bars.

"Now, Professor—"

A dull flush rolled up under his tan. "You can't mean to publicize this humiliation!"

"Humiliation?" She frowned in amazement. Jack wasn't normally so dense. "Far from it. We're crusaders for the truth, investigating serious concerns at great risk to life and limb, battling the system for freedom of information. We're the lead story!"

"Oh, no, count me out!"

"Can't do it." She lifted her shoulders in apology. "Public's right to know."

"Yeah," Lauren interjected, giving a sage nod from the other side of the cage. "Ciel's a real stickler for that."

Jack groaned heavily and jammed a hand through his hair. "Do you know what this kind of thing can do to me? Arrested, a possible jail sentence, fines, and my reputation straight down the toilet! The grant committee—"

"Should be impressed!" Ciel grinned, elation bubbling. "Don't you see? We're onto something big, and Sonny Prejean's up to his fat neck in whatever it is. Why else would he press all sorts of charges, insist the sheriff throw the book at us, and threaten a lawsuit to boot? All I did was climb a fence. Talk about your overreaction!"

Jack narrowed his eyes. "You're letting your imagination run wild again. Prejean's just a businessman who's reached his limit with this UFO craziness, and I can't say that I blame him—I'm getting there myself."

Ciel realized that he was seething at her. Well, maybe

she had sort of talked him into exploring Prejean's place, but he hadn't been too hard to convince. Still, it looked as though she was going to be the one to take the rap again. With a gulp, she hastened to defend herself.

"It's the grand tradition of newspapering, Jack. We're Woodward and Bernstein! Can't you see that?"

"The only thing I see is that I'm behind another two days' work, and if I don't focus on what I need to do, my career is shot!"

"But we can't give up now," she protested. Frustration and dismay clouded her expression. "We're close to some answers. I can smell it!"

"Look, if you insist on pursuing this, you'll have to play bloodhound by yourself."

"You aren't going to help me?"

His features turned stony. "No."

She gasped in disappointment. Just when she'd believed he could put aside his orthodox thinking and become a dreamer, just when she needed him most. "But, Jack—"

"Here we go, folks." Sheaf of papers in hand, Cleveland rattled keys, unlocked the holding cell and waved them out. "Sorry it took so long. Dr. Cooper, if you'll just sign..."

"With pleasure." Grim-lipped, Jack paused at the office counter and scrawled his signature on the bottom of a document. "All right if I go now?"

"Sure. You'll be assigned a court date in a few days."

"Swell." He turned toward the door and rushed out.

Cleveland thrust another document at Ciel. "You next, Ciel."

Ciel groaned in dismay and darted after Jack. "Professor, wait!"

Cleveland caught her shirttail, hauled her back.

"Whoa. You gotta sign this, Ciel. And Lauren, I need you to witness both of these...."

Hastily, Ciel scribbled her name, then ran after Jack, catching up with him on the sidewalk outside. "Jack, wait up!"

Wearily, he passed a hand over his eyes. "I need some space to think, Ciel."

"All right, I understand that. Things have been a bit bizarre between us, I'll admit."

"A bit?" He blew out a breath of pure exasperation.

"Well, like in *Cosmic Monsters*—"

"No!" He pointed a finger at her nose. "No more. No more aliens, no more off-the-wall harebrained Ciel Landry ideas! I've had all I can take!"

Her lip trembled, and she bit it hard. "Yes, Jack."

"Good. Just so you understand."

"I understand you might be feeling a little... overwhelmed at the moment, but putting aside anything personal we have, I need your professional help, now more than ever."

He rounded on her, his features hard. "Damn it, I've got problems of my own, or had you forgotten?"

"But the fish kill. You said—"

"My first priority has to be to my grant project. Only, somehow I forgot that." His eyes were flat and coppery with accusation.

Ciel's heart sank. He blamed her. His look all but shouted that she was a bad influence, destructive to his peace of mind and career. *But what about us?* her heart demanded. What about the loving and laughter and tenderness—didn't that count for anything in Jack Cooper's logbook?

She didn't want to believe he was so unfeeling that what they'd shared meant nothing to him. Or was he running away, ranting about projects and priorities because it had meant too much? He'd been up-front about the limits of their relationship from the very first, so did hanging on to that kind of hope make her a fool, or just a woman in love?

Ciel swallowed hard as her heart tightened. She was in love with him, head over heels, fly-me-to-the-moon in love. And he was looking at her as though he never wanted to see her again! She had to find a way to keep them connected somehow, until he had a chance to get over his pique and realize just what they had together.

"What about all those samples you took?" she asked carefully. "I can send Kyle after the boat. You never struck me as the kind of man to leave something undone."

His jaw worked under the shadow of his stubble. "Fine. Bring them on, and I'll send them to the lab, for all the good it'll do. But I'm through with this so-called investigation. You can make yourself a laughingstock. I've got more important things to do."

"You're not the least bit curious about what's behind that fence at Prejean Oil?"

"I can't afford it. Understand this about me once and for all, Ciel. My work comes first—always."

It was a warning, pure and simple. *Don't care too much. Don't expect more than I'm willing to give. Don't come to close.*

Icy disappointment chilled Ciel's soul. How did you batter down such walls? She reached deep for courage. So love wasn't for the faint of heart. What else was new?

Squaring her shoulders, Ciel acknowledged that priorities were very fine things to have, but Jack Cooper wasn't the only one with goals and aspirations. And now she had two primary ones—to help this mutton-headed man realize that loving her was something he *could* do, and to prove to the world that Ciel Landry was one hell of an investigative reporter.

"We're more alike than you'd like to think, Professor," she murmured. "So I guess we'll both just do what we have to."

9

"DADGUMIT, MAMA. Another woman I could compete with, but pond scum?"

"Surely it's not as bad as that, *chère*." Marie poured another cup of black-as-Mississippi-mud coffee and passed it across the kitchen table to her daughter. "I can't imagine anyone mistaking you for a fungus."

"Algae, Mama. Jack's studying algae."

"Whatever."

Freshly showered, wrapped in a checkered cotton robe, Ciel sipped the potent brew and tried to throw off the aftereffects of a night in the wilderness and what Marie had begun to refer to as her "unfortunate incarceration." The television blared from the den, where Kyle and Tony kibitzed over which game show model was the most beautiful. It was barely midmorning, but Ciel felt as though she'd been up a week, and there was still the paper to get out.

She sighed and ran a hand through her damp ringlets. "After everything that's happened, I'm sure the only way Jack would be looking more charitably on me is if I really were a one-celled organism. He's convinced that's the size of my brain anyway."

"You're too hard on yourself." Marie peered over the rim of her coffee mug, her dark eyes keenly observant. "You like him a lot, don't you?"

Ciel drew a fingertip through a drop of spilled coffee

and traced moist patterns on the tabletop. She could never hide anything from her mother. "Does it show that much?"

Marie reached across the table and patted her hand. "Only to me, *chère*. I'm not prying into your business. You're a big girl, only I don't want to see you get hurt."

"It may be too late for that," Ciel admitted. She bit her lower lip to still a sudden tremor, then risked a wry smile. "Maybe Jack won't think I belong in the loony bin if I can figure out what's going on around here. But I'm blocked at every step—the mayor's edict, trespassing charges, and now Jack's saying he's too busy to help, when I know the scientist in him was intrigued. Oh, it's too frustrating!"

"So you're giving up?"

Ciel looked askance at her mother. "Of course not! This may be the only crack I get at investigative reporting, so I'm going to give it my best shot."

"That's my girl."

"Only, where to start..." Ciel tapped a thoughtful forefinger against her chin.

"Is not!"

"Is too! She beats Vanna like a rug."

In cutoffs and T-shirts, Kyle and Tony invaded the kitchen, helping themselves to glasses of orange juice as they continued a heated discussion of the merits of various TV spokesmodels.

"You boys going to need your usual quota of alien blood today?" Marie asked mildly, interrupting the ruckus.

"I guess not, Aunt Marie." Tony looked at his older cousin for confirmation.

"Yeah, thanks anyway, Mama." Wiping away an orange mustache with his shirttail, Kyle nodded. "We're shutting down the pop stand. There's not enough business since they've closed off the lookout point.''

"It's plain dumb of Emile to shut down a booming tourist attraction without so much as a by-your-leave." Ciel drummed fingertips against the table impatiently. "It's the best summer the local merchants have ever had, not to mention the advertising business it's generated for the *Press,* and our own mayor stifles it because of a little traffic congestion!"

"What else would you expect from a shortsighted ignoramus like Emile?" Marie asked. "I could do a better job in my sleep."

Ciel laughed, and her eyes danced with mischief. "What we need is another close encounter to stir things up, get those cash registers ringing again. That would fix Emile's little red wagon!"

"Yeah! And maybe the TV people would come back and interview me and Tony about our alien blood," Kyle said eagerly. "I could even tell 'em my joke. What do you get when you cross a galaxy with a toad frog, Ciel?"

"I haven't the foggiest."

"Star warts!"

"Oh, please..."

"Wait, here's another one—if an athlete gets athlete's foot, and a tennis pro gets tennis elbow, what does Dr. Cooper the astronaut get?"

"Beats me."

"Missile toe!" Tony shouted, and the boys doubled over with hilarity.

"Enough, you two!" Ciel rolled her eyes. "Anyway, I suppose two extraterrestrial visits in one summer is too much to expect."

Tony sobered and his brow furrowed. "You really believe it was aliens, Ciel?"

She thought about all the unusual occurrences she'd catalogued. Coincidence? Summer heat? And that strange light at Jack's camp. Her own fevered imagination? The only thing she really knew was that she couldn't stick her head in the sand like an ostrich and ignore it all. She gave Tony a wry shrug.

"Your guess is as good as mine, but I'm trying to find out for sure. Since you fellows aren't busy, will you take Aunt Tee-Ta's bass boat and fetch the bateau for me? There're a bunch of sample bags and bottles that I want you to deliver to Dr. Cooper."

Kyle nodded. "Sure. We were wanting to do some fishing anyway."

"You be careful now, you hear?" Marie warned. "Wouldn't want you to get lost."

A devilish glint sparked in Kyle's eyes. "Don't worry, Mama. We aren't as dumb as some grown-ups."

Pretending to be highly insulted, Ciel tossed her napkin at him. "Hey, watch it, you Klingon!"

"Oh, yeah? So when you suck face with your *boyfriend* who likes *pond scum,* what does that make you?"

"Kyle!" Ciel choked, somewhere between laughter and total embarrassment. "You've been spying on me?"

Her brother's eyes got wide. "Oops. Gotta go get that boat. Come on, Tony!"

The two boys scrambled out the back door. Ciel buried her hot face in her hands and moaned.

"This family! Is nothing sacred?"

"Only our devotion to foolishness." Marie smiled. "And it will be a sad day when we can't find a single thing to laugh about."

"Amen." Ciel knew her mother was right. None of the problems before her was insurmountable if she just kept her perspective and her sense of humor. Jack wasn't

the stodgy professor he'd been when he first arrived at
her doorstep, and she knew that it was due at least in
part to her. He'd get over this latest fiasco, and then
they'd see where they were going.

Feeling more hopeful, Ciel pushed to her feet and
dropped a swift peck on Marie's cheek. "Thanks,
Mama. You always know just what to say."

"Like get to work?"

Ciel chuckled. "Exactly. So sit back and watch me
put together a newspaper that'll make this little town sit
up and take notice!"

"COONS DO NOT play tic-tac-toe," Miss Wendolyn Marchon informed Ciel solemnly. A spinster in her sixties,
she taught seventh grade, owned six cats and drove a
new sports car every year. She stood for no nonsense in
her classroom or her truck patch.

"Yes'm." Ciel scribbled the edict in her notebook.

"Especially not on cantaloupes."

"No, ma'am." The vines in Miss Marchon's well-
tended cantaloupe patch were as pretty as a picture, with
their tendrils, the ground laden with a multitude of
golden melons ripening in the August heat.

"They didn't miss one."

"I can see that," Ciel said. Indeed, each and every
melon sported markings etched into its hide that resem-
bled hieroglyphics. Or hen's scratching. Take your pick.

"Ruined a perfectly good crop." Miss Marchon
sniffed indignantly. "Reckon it's some sort of code? A
message from beyond the stars?"

"Miss Marchon, all I can say is if raccoons did this
we've got some awfully smart critters in Whiskey Bay."

"WATCH OUT! There goes another one!"

The overhead streetlight on Evangeline Street gave a
muffled *pop*.

"Criminy!" Ciel held her notebook over her head and dodged as a hail of flying light-bulb fragments hit the ground beside her. All up and down the quiet residential neighborhood, shards littered the sidewalks and yards.

Utility supervisor Everett Waskins held on to his hard hat and looked worried. "Can't keep a single bulb going on this entire street."

"Surely it's just some sort of power surge, Everett."

"That's what you'd think. But none of the readings is off. It's almost as if someone were taking target practice."

"What do you plan to do?"

"Beats the heck out of me. We've tried everything I can think of."

"But this is dangerous!"

"I'll say. The residents are out to lynch me!"

"I guess you could just take out all the light bulbs until things settle down."

Everett's face lit up with pure relief. "Ciel, that's it! Now, why didn't I think of that?"

PAIR NABBED AT Local Business

In Ciel's shabby garage office, Jack stared at the latest issue of the *Press,* groaned, swore, then washed another aspirin down with a swallow of water.

Damn Ciel's hide! His own face—from the official NASA crew photo, no less—smiled back up at him. To be fair, Ciel had also included an unflattering mug shot of herself. Their crime and subsequent arrest were described in lurid detail. The fish kill, the curious occurrences still happening around the parish and the fact that when questioned "Prejean Oil refused comment" were all there. Red ink announced "Final Frontier Days" sales inside this edition.

Praying no one in Houston would get wind of this debacle, Jack crumpled the paper and tossed it in the wastebasket. If he could have gotten his hands on Ciel at that moment, he'd have cheerfully committed mayhem! No, that wasn't true. As annoyed as he was at the story, there was only one thing he'd really like to do with her, and the carnal image made his groin tighten and his blood steam. The fact was, he'd never felt so hungry for a woman in all his life.

He hadn't even seen her, except at a distance, since Tuesday morning. After realizing that he and Ciel simply marched to two different drummers, he'd thought it best to put distance between them. Besides, his departure for his home base in Houston was growing closer by the day. So why put off the inevitable?

Since the things that went bump in the night at the camp were working overtime again and he couldn't sleep anyway, he'd toiled nonstop for two days, and his preliminary data were finally coming together. Logic said any further complications with his and Ciel's short-term relationship should be avoided at all costs. But all the logical reasoning and desire for emotional detachment in the world didn't alter the fact that he was missing her like hell.

And not just the physical side of their relationship, either, fantastic as it was. No, he missed her smile, her laughter, her warmth and the way it melted the icy shell in which he'd encased his heart. It was a mistake, a weakness he couldn't allow, and it scared the bejesus out of him.

Grinding his teeth in frustration, Jack threw himself down and began tapping away again at the computer keyboard. He gave himself a shake, irritated to find his movements almost furtive. So what if this wasn't his algae project? If he chose to construct a computer model containing Ciel's observations about summer madness in Whiskey Bay and his notes on dead fish and some obscure soil and water samples, it certainly wasn't out of any sense of responsibility to Ciel and her crazy notions.

Yeah, Cooper, and the moon is made of bean dip and you're elected to bring the chips!

Jack grimaced and scrubbed his jaw with his palms. Hell, what did his motivation matter? Maybe he was feeling guilty. Maybe he was simply curious. Maybe he just wanted to help. His lips tightened. He only hoped Ciel didn't misinterpret his interest.

Someone scratched on the door. "Jack? I saw your light. May I come in?"

Ciel! Pleasure rolled over him like a tidal wave. The raw, uncontrollable power of it surprised him, making him instantly defensive. He tamped down the feeling, exchanging it for wariness and a certain little measure of belligerence as he opened the door.

"That's a stupid question, sunshine. I—" He frowned. "What's wrong?"

Under the yellow bug light illuminating the landing, she looked a trifle uncertain and utterly weary, her flyaway curls in a barrette at her nape, her slacks and gingham shirt rumpled. Only the crystal pendant she wore seemed as brilliant as usual.

"I hate to disturb you..."

"This is your place, for God's sake. You don't even have to knock." Impatient, worried, he ushered her inside, inspecting her as he did so. She appeared so tired and fragile, and the need to protect her, to hold her close, was almost irresistible. Folding his arms, he resisted. "You look like hell."

Her lips twisted wryly. "You really know how to sweet-talk a girl, Professor. I've been up since five. Someone broke into the *Press* office last night."

"What!" He shoved fingers through his hair. "Burglars?"

She shrugged. "The sheriff thinks it was just some kids. Nothing important was missing, and they didn't damage any equipment, just left an unholy mess to clean up."

"Then it could have been worse."

"Oh, yes. Of course, Lauren's ticked because she got left to do the straightening up when the call came in over the scanner about the saucer burns in the Williamses' driveway. Then there was Miss Marchon's cantaloupe patch, and all the streetlights on Evangeline Boulevard mysteriously quit working last night, but Angie Turner's porch lights won't go off at all now. Then Lucky Hyde cut down a pine and found Lincoln's profile in the tree rings—"

"Whoa!" Jack held up his hands. "Saucer burns?"

"Well, that's what Cleveland called them."

"You mean the hysteria is starting up again?"

She licked her lips, her eyes wary. "Uh, all I know is, I've been called out about fifty times today to look at some pretty unusual stuff."

"This town is unbelievable!" Jack shook his head in disgust. "Everyone in it ought to be committed."

"Don't blame me—I didn't do it!" She tilted her chin. "Anyway, no one's asking you to make like Ripley and believe it or not. I just came by to see if you have anything on those fish and water samples yet."

He hesitated, then gestured reluctantly at the computer. "The lab reports won't come in until tomorrow, but I'm collating data now."

"You are?" Surprise brightened her blue eyes, and a pleased smile tugged the corners of her mouth. "Shouldn't you be working on your project?"

His expression turned mulish. "I was taking a break, okay?"

With a half smile that caught at his heart, she stepped close, laying her hand against his chest.

"It's more than okay. It's downright heroic considering your circumstances. Thank you, Jack."

Her touch was like an electric shock. Wrapping his fingers around her wrist, he tugged her closer, knowing this was a mistake, unable to help himself. "Ciel..."

Her lips parted, and she caught her breath on a little gulp. Encouraged, he bent his head, fastening his mouth to hers. She tasted of spice and honey, and he groaned, famished for her, unable to get enough of her. Burying his hands in her sunset-colored curls, he held her still and feasted, as a man long-denied nourishment and suddenly set before a banquet.

She hummed, approval and acceptance in the tone, her lips pliant and clinging, her body melting against his. Tongues dueled, chasing delight in sinuous interplay. Jack felt her tremble with need and excitement, and his hunger exploded.

He transferred his attentions to the side of her neck, laving the freckles with his tongue. She threw her head back, allowing him greater access, her breasts rising and falling with her rapid exhalations. Enticed, he palmed the lush mounds, kneading gently, and was rewarded when she moaned.

Jack's voice was hoarse, his breathing ragged. "Ah, sunshine, I've missed you..."

"Good. I hope you've been miserable without your Daring Blonde around." She gasped and gripped his shoulders as his thumbs brushed her nipples through her clothing.

"So you're trying to tell me you like driving me insane?"

A strange, shaky laugh burbled from her throat, bittersweet and tender all at once. "Oh, Jack, you idiot. I'm trying to tell you I'm in love with you."

Startled, he raised his head, his eyes shadowed. "Ciel, I..."

She touched her fingers to his lips. "No, don't say anything. There were never any promises or guarantees. But I want you to know I intend to make it very hard for you to walk away from this, from me...."

"You're making it damned near impossible," he muttered, his words harsh with frustration and guilt and burning need. He took her mouth again, almost ruthlessly, hoping somehow to assuage the hunger and deny it all at once, but it was futile. And her response was so immediate, so full and loving, he was lost, cast adrift in the splendor that only Ciel could bring to him.

Alarms sounded in his head, pealing and shrieking in warning. Lights flashed behind his eyes, harbingers of disaster. He wanted her desperately, but she deserved better. Their lives didn't mesh. She was so...impulsive, impetuous, so unpredictable. And so generous and giving and honest it made him ashamed. He couldn't hope to keep her, but how could he let her go?

And then she was taking the choice from him, pushing back, tearing her lips from his, and he felt his heart being ripped from his body.

"Ciel, please," he murmured, desperate. "Don't go..."

"Jack, look!" Struggling, she twisted in his grasp. "My God, what is it—the mother ship?"

He came back to reality with a jolt. The office revolved with blue and white lights, like the inside of a kaleidoscope gone mad, and the air reverberated with unearthly wails. For a wild instant, he actually believed in alien invaders and spaceships, but when Ciel slipped free and rushed toward the door, sanity returned and he was right on her heels.

Blue lights rotating, sirens howling, a sheriff's patrol car rolled into the Landry driveway. Ciel was halfway down the stairs when it came to a halt. Marie appeared under the light on the back porch of the house, holding the screen door open with one hand and shielding her eyes with the other.

As Jack and Ciel stumbled off the garage staircase, Deputy Cleveland Henderson heaved his large bulk from the driver's seat of the car. His expression was grim.

"'Evening, Cleveland," Marie called uncertainly. "Something we can do for you?"

"Miz Landry." With a curt nod, Cleveland opened the back door of the patrol car and hauled out two white-faced twelve-year-olds by the scruffs of their T-shirts. "You know these two?"

"Kyle! Tony!" Hurrying down the back steps, Marie joined Ciel and Jack at the car, her face pinched with concern.

"What happened?" Ciel demanded. "Are they hurt?"

Cleveland thrust the two boys forward. "No, ma'am, but I'm sorry to say they're under arrest."

Marie drew a shocked breath, and Ciel caught her mother's arm to support her.

"What's the charge, Officer?" Jack demanded, eyeing the youngsters dubiously.

He knew a little about the law's capriciousness after his own recent experience. Chastened, Kyle and Tony kept their eyes on the scruffy toes of their athletic shoes, their whole attitude one of extreme guilt.

Cleveland, mouth stern, began reciting. "Misdemeanor mischief, trespassing, destruction of private property—"

"My God, what have you boys done?" Marie gasped.

"Pretended to be Martians, that's what," the deputy answered. "Found 'em making scorch patterns on the old tennis courts with a propane torch, just like the ones in the Williamses' driveway. Admitted they dragged a garbage can on a rope to flatten a circle in the Buswells' truck patch. Made floating objects appear out on Cemetery Road with fishing line and flashlights. Yes, sir, I'd say that we've finally found the answer to Whiskey Bay's 'alien' problem!"

"All the things that have been going on—they're responsible?" Jack asked incredulously.

"Looks that way," Cleveland said.

Her face tight with embarrassment and fury, Marie twisted her fingers in her youngest son's shirt and gave him a shake. "Explain, young man. *Now*."

Dragging the toe of his shoe through the gravel, Kyle gave his mother a pleading look from under his dark bangs. "We were just trying to help Ciel."

His sister started visibly. "Help me? How?"

"You said what we needed was another alien visit." Tony gulped, looking close to tears. "So we made one."

"Darned convincing, too," Cleveland said. "Had us chasing all over the parish for the past two days answering calls. Some folks were getting flat hysterical. It'll be a relief when word gets round that it was just a kid's prank."

"If that's all it was," Jack muttered, ugly suspicion sucking at him like a whirlpool. Ciel read the accusation in his eyes and drew a sharp breath.

"You don't for one minute think I had anything to do with this."

"Well, did you?" he blurted.

The contempt in her voice flayed him. "Believe what you like. You will anyway."

Jack would have given anything at that moment to call back his hasty words, but she'd already turned on her heel and stalked toward the house. Dismayed, he stared after her.

"I figured I'd best bring the boys home tonight, Miz Landry," Cleveland was saying. "If you'll let Tony's mother know what's going on and vouch for them in the meantime, we'll get things officially sorted out in the morning."

"Thank you, Deputy. I'll call Tee-Ta right now." Marie grabbed both boys in a Vulcan neck pinch that would have made Mr. Spock proud. Her lips trembled with the effort to control herself. "Have you got anything to say before I ground you for life, Kyle Landry?"

"Aw, Mama!" Squirming, Kyle shot Jack a pleading look. "You tell her, Dr. Cooper."

Jack dragged his gaze back from Ciel's retreating figure. "Tell her what?"

"Being a jailbird ain't so bad!"

NEWS IN a little Southern town spreads like wildfire, especially between editions of the weekly paper. Still, nothing could have prepared Ciel for the consequences of the Whiskey Bay grapevine.

By nine o'clock the next morning, word had gone out among Tee-Ta's Rook Club members that the Whiskey

Bay sighting was a hoax concocted by two adolescent males.

Darling boys, and so precocious! Imagine pulling the wool over everyone's eyes like that!

By ten o'clock, the first campers were pulling up stakes along Ballard Road.

Nothing to this flying saucer thing. Knew it all the time!

By half past ten, no less than seven relatives, friends and acquaintances, including Izzy Chaston, had called Ciel to ask if it was true that she'd put the boys up to their mischief and/or emphatically state that they didn't believe a word of the rumor.

Just call you "Ma Barker" from now on. Trespassing, gangs, what next...bank robbery?

By eleven-thirty, Mayor Emile Nabors had come by the *Press* office, ostensibly to turn in a news release praising the effectiveness of the Whiskey Bay police in dealing with the juvenile offenders, but really to gloat.

You and that fancy-pants NASA guy want the name of a good lawyer?

By 1:00 p.m. a steady stream of RVs, campers, portable hotdog stands, tour buses, crafts concessionaires and even Sister Inez with her camouflage tent loaded in her trunk were making an exodus along Main Street like the Israelites leaving Egypt.

Someone saw Elvis delivering singing telegrams around Vicksburg—let's go have a look-see!

By 2:00 p.m. Lauren had broken not one, but two nails answering the phone and thirty-six town merchants had canceled their "Shoot the Moon" ads in next week's paper.

Sorry, Ciel—but how about a two-dollar want ad?

So when Jack walked into the *Press* offices at a quarter to four, eyes hidden behind his Ray-Ban sunglasses, Ciel wasn't necessarily surprised. Despite the way her heart leaped at the sight of him, lean and handsome in his faded jeans and space shuttle *Columbia* shirt, she still felt put upon by his suspicions of the night before, and so, as she greeted him over the counter, her voice was cool.

"May I help you?"

Jack dragged the wire stems from behind his ears and flicked a look at Lauren, who was busy sorting a stack of canceled ad orders at the computer table. Never short on brains despite her sexpot looks, Lauren took the hint.

"Um, maybe I'll just take these to the back." With an encouraging wink for Ciel, Lauren sashayed out of earshot.

Jack fixed his eyes on Ciel. "You're not still ticked, are you?"

"Oh, because the man I'm involved with thinks I'd stoop to enticing children into criminal activities just to keep a story alive? That someone important to me believes my journalistic integrity is on a level with some tabloid?" She tilted her chin. "What do you think, Professor?"

"That I'm being condemned for one tiny moment of doubt." He raised his hands at her scowl. "For God's sake, sunshine, you've had me on a roller coaster since the moment we met. Can I help it if I get a little rattled sometimes?"

"So it's all my fault?" She jammed her hands into the pockets of her denim skirt and glared at him. "If that's the best you can do, maybe you'd better go."

"Oh, *hell*." Leaning over the counter, he caught her chin and kissed her hard.

She wrenched free, hating the way her heart hammered against her chest wall at his merest touch. Anger made her splutter. "What *is* your problem?"

"You, lady," he growled. "And the fact that the Ken and Barbie of local TV have been breathing down my neck all day, trying to interview me about a certain red-haired reporter, trespassing charges and what the media are now calling 'The Great Flying Saucer Hoax'—a phenomenon, rumor has it, of which I have intimate knowledge, only I'm under orders from the U.S. government to maintain strict silence."

Ciel's eyes widened. "Oh, Lord."

"Oh, yes. And the moment the grant committee gets wind of this, I'll be laughed right out of competition."

"They wouldn't be so unfair." She bit her lip, uncertain. "Would they?"

"Sometimes a scientist's greatest fear is not being taken seriously. If I'm perceived as a lightweight..." He shrugged. "Even in the fairest competition, prejudice like that can make a critical difference."

A pang of dismay pierced her, and she reached for his hand. "Oh, Jack, all your work—"

The office door slammed open with a reverberating *whack,* and a wiry man with a thatch of gray hair and Ross Perot ears stampeded inside.

"Ciel Landry!" he barked.

"Mr. Crenshaw." Ciel's mouth fell open she was so astounded. Her boss never put foot on the premises if he could help it. "What are you doing here?"

"What I should have done months ago." He plucked a black-and-orange For Sale sign from the revolving rack and slammed it down on the counter in front of her. "Put that in the window. And the *Whiskey Bay Press* ceases publication with this issue."

Ciel gasped as if he'd punched her in the stomach,

barely aware of Jack's dark scowl and Lauren's appearance behind her. "What? But, sir—!"

"Can't tolerate yellow journalism," Crenshaw snapped. "Won't have it. Got the reputation of my other papers to consider. One rogue reporter ruins 'em all."

"Mr. Crenshaw, I only tried to report the truth."

"Your own brother, flying saucers and Prejean Oil threatening to sue me for all I'm worth—no, ma'am, I'm not taking any chances. And word's out you honestly believe we've got little E.T.s flitting around causing all this trouble. Well, crazy lady, you're done making mischief for me!"

"You've got no right to blame Ciel," Lauren said, her dark eyes flashing. "Admit it, you've just been looking for any excuse to close us down and you've latched onto this!"

"I don't have to admit anything, missy," Crenshaw retorted, his ears turning red. "By the way, you're fired, too."

"Too late," Lauren snapped, slamming the stack of bills onto the counter and grabbing up her shoulder bag. "I quit, you old skinflint! Just in time, too, 'cause Tiny and I are expecting."

"Lauren, ohmigosh, how wonderful!" Ciel blinked. "I mean, it's terrible about your job. Mr. Crenshaw, you can't do this—"

"Just watch me."

"Don't worry, Ciel. I'm really looking forward to staying home and being Mama. Ya'll come see me in my rocking chair!" Head high, Lauren flashed a brilliant smile at Jack and sauntered out of the office.

"Hussy." Crenshaw gave the place a brief inspection, dismissed the *Press* with one final glance of distaste, then headed for the door himself. "I'll send someone after the equipment next week. And sweep up around this place before you go, will you?"

The door slammed behind Crenshaw. Ciel staggered back and sat down with a thump in Lauren's typesetting chair. For a dizzy moment she couldn't catch her breath, and her skin felt cold and clammy.

Vaulting the counter, Jack took one look, then pushed her head between her knees. "Breathe."

She followed orders, straightening after a few minutes with a shaky smile. "I'm okay. Whew, I wasn't expecting that. Didn't even have time to call in the army before Godzilla flattened Tokyo."

"God, I'm sorry, Ciel." Concern drew his brows together. "What will you do?"

"I don't know. I guess I'll have time to devote to my novel now, won't I?" She shoved trembling fingers through her curls, and her features hardened with determination. "But I have a job to finish first. There're still a lot of questions—"

He growled in exasperation. "Look, will you just give it up already? It's over."

"Jack, you don't understand. I grilled the boys—yes, they pulled a few stunts, but they weren't responsible for the first landing site or the fish kill. And they didn't vandalize this office, either. Something still doesn't smell right."

He rose to his feet, rubbing his nape in exasperation. "And I've got more important things to do than get involved in your screwball schemes again."

It stung that he could so easily dismiss her, give so little credence to what she thought was important. "So who's asking you to?"

"Can't you let it go? Put it all down to summer UFO madness and have done with it?"

"Just forget it, huh?" Blue eyes burning, she stood and raked him with a glance that radiated disappointment. "Be just like you, never digging any deeper than the surface because you're too afraid of what you might find or what it might force you to admit or feel?"

"What's that supposed to mean?"

"You figure it out."

Baffled, he stared at her. "Lady, do you come with an instruction book? You never make sense!"

"Thank you very much, Professor." Her voice was tight with hurt and wounded pride. "And don't worry, I won't involve you in any more of my screwball schemes. So why don't you just go and get on with all that *important* work of yours? We wouldn't want to keep mankind waiting, would we? And I've got sweeping up to do."

"Fine." He started toward the door, his jaw taut with annoyance.

"Fine." She snatched a broom from behind a desk and began to whisk furiously at the dirty floor.

Jack opened his mouth to say something else, then thought better of it. Back ramrod straight, he headed out the door, joining the last of the raucous cavalcade pouring out of Whiskey Bay, leaving it as empty as a ghost town.

Drat the man! The broom stirred clouds of dust into the air, but Ciel was too furious to sneeze. Who made Jack Cooper the authority on the universe? Give it up, ha! It was a free country, and officially employed or not, she could pursue her investigation if she wanted to.

Except Jack was the only one with any real, concrete information. Ciel frowned, then brightened. And that was information he'd just happened to place in Ciel's own computer! Maybe that was where she should start.

She was going to get to the bottom of all the strange goings-on in Whiskey Bay if it killed her!

It nearly did.

By midnight, Ciel gave up trying to make heads or tails of Jack's reports. She rose from her computer, ducking her head to miss the single bulb dangling from its frayed cord, rubbing her tired back and gritty eyes. Mind reeling with arcane scientific language, she knew if she could just put one or two pieces together everything would make sense. Maybe.

Jack would know what it all meant. If only he'd help by answering a few questions. Heck, he owed her! And it wouldn't take but a few minutes of his precious time. Leaving everything just as it was, she hurried downstairs, snagging a flashlight hanging on the rack in the garage.

Before she could consider the wisdom of approaching Jack about the subject yet again, she was jogging through the dark down the well-beaten path to Uncle Etienne's camp, the secret, fertile scent of the bayou filling her head. Before she could lose her nerve, she was knocking on the camp-house door.

Jack pushed open the screen door, a sexy and sleep-rumpled phantom with eyes like a hungry lion's.

"You have something you want to say, sunshine?"

She took a deep breath. "Take me to your leader?"

10

IT WAS a puzzle, a conundrum of fish and flying saucers and floating vats of slime. The images drifted in Ciel's drowsy brain, half dream, half reality, and she teetered on the verge of understanding, knowing if she could just put the pieces together it would all be clear.

Something gently shook her, exhorting her to wake. Warm lips nuzzled her ear, tracked the smattering of freckles down her neck, and the dream dissolved, forgotten in a shiver of delicious sensation.

Murmuring with pleasure, Ciel smiled in the darkness, rolling closer to Jack. Languid, sated, still naked and tangled in the tender aftermath of loving, they cuddled on the cool, rumpled sheets. Her heart full, Ciel touched his face, loving him with every fiber of her being, praying that with her care Jack's defenses would eventually fall and he'd know that he loved her, too.

Until then, nothing else truly mattered. Not his project, or the loss of her job, or the hundred unanswered questions surrounding Whiskey Bay. No, not even pond scum, or adventures in the Brazilian rain forest, or Sylvie Fairstar, or the scent of smoke wafting on the humid air—

Ciel's eyes flew open, the faint, acrid aroma in her nostrils, on her tongue. With a gasp, she flung herself out of the bed.

"Ciel?" Raised on one elbow, Jack was a dark silhouette. "What's wrong?"

She pressed her palms against the windowpanes. Through the distance, back along the path she'd taken earlier, veiled behind the moss-hung trees, an evil orange reflection flickered against the night sky.

"Fire," she breathed. "My God—Mama, Kyle!"

Minutes later, half-dressed, panic-stricken, her lungs nearly exploding, Ciel burst out of the path into the backyard, with Jack at her side. With a surge of relief that made her light-headed and giddy, Ciel took in the situation—the house unscathed, the garage engulfed in crimson and tangerine flames, her mother and brother holding each other in the side yard as the Whiskey Bay Volunteer Fire Department pulled hoses and sprayed water. Someone had managed to move the cars well back out of harm's way.

"Mama!" Stumbling, Ciel rushed forward. Kyle noticed her first, punched his mother and pointed.

Marie spun around, enveloping her daughter in a frantic hug. "Oh, *merci le bon Dieu!* I was afraid you were inside…"

"No, Mama," Ciel soothed. "I was at Jack's. I'm sorry you worried. I'm sorry…"

"It doesn't matter now, *chère*. We're all safe, that's all that counts."

Ciel nodded as her mother released her, surprised to find that she was shaking all over. Grim lines bracketing his mouth, Jack cupped her shoulders and pulled her close, her back against his chest. Gratefully, she accepted his strength.

With a scream of tearing rafters, the old wooden garage chose that moment to collapse in on itself, sending a shower of crimson sparks into the black sky and the volunteer firemen scurrying back for cover. Chief Clemon Wyandotte, sweating in his billed hat and slicker, stamped over to them.

"Sorry, Miz Landry. Hoped we could save it, but..."

"Just don't let it spread to the house, Clemon."

"No, ma'am, don't worry. We'll have it under control in no time. How you suppose it started?"

Ciel felt the blood run from her face. "It's my fault," she whispered. "I left everything on. That old wiring...I knew better...oh, God!"

"Well, it's going to be a total loss." Clemon started toward the pumper truck, and Marie and Tony trailed after him for a closer look. He called back over his shoulder to Ciel. "Hope you got insurance on the important stuff."

Important stuff. Ciel choked suddenly, her stomach going weightless as the world dropped from under her feet. Jack's notes and computer disks, her unfinished manuscript, the Whiskey Bay sighting files, even her notebook—they were all inside the crackling conflagration! Twisting around, she gave Jack a horrified look, her voice a croak.

"Jack, your project. Where—"

The muscle in his jaw throbbing visibly, he inclined his head toward the burning pile. "There."

"All of it?" Desperation and guilt and despair made her frantic. "What about backup files at the camp house?"

He shook his head, his eyes bleak and devastated as his life's work went up in smoke. "My stupidity. The files, the hard copies, all the data in the computer—I brought everything over here just yesterday to finish up."

"Oh, no." Her throat constricted. "Can...can you reconstruct it?"

"Start over with the old research I left in Houston?" He shook his head. "No, not in time. I'm finished."

"Oh, God." She pressed knuckles to her mouth. "I'm sorry. It's my fault. If only I'd listened to you, I wouldn't have even been working in the office tonight and none of this would be happening. Let me help. There's got to be something...what can I do?"

"Nothing!" His voice was like a whip. "For God's sake, don't try to help me any more. Haven't you done enough damage?"

The answer was yes.

Awash with remorse, Ciel staggered under the awful realization. She finally understood Jack was right, his reservations about their relationship absolutely valid.

As desperately as she loved him, she was the wrong kind of woman for him. From the word go, she'd embarrassed him, made him uncomfortable, forced him into roles he neither appreciated nor enjoyed. His involvement with her had put his professional reputation on the line, threatened to turn him into a laughingstock with his peers and jeopardized his livelihood. Now, due to her carelessness and impetuosity, she'd reduced his work to ashes and sabotaged his future. In short, she'd taken everything Jack had ever cherished and turned it into disaster, into a bad B movie!

All in the name of love. Because she'd selfishly, blindly, thought she knew what was best for him. It was clear she'd been sadly mistaken, and it had cost Jack everything he cared about.

What a monumental child she was, believing in aliens, dreaming her wild dreams! How utterly stupid, and how disillusioning to realize she'd never really grown up. But it was high time she did, if only to prove she could do the right thing. And Ciel knew in that moment that if she truly loved Jack, then there was only one thing she could do.

Smoke burned her eyes, and tears overflowed, scalding her face, her soul. "I'm so sorry for everything, Jack," she said, choking. "I wish to heaven there were some way I could make it all up to you, but you're right, I've hurt you enough."

In the flickering orange light, his handsome features looked carved from stone. At the sight of her tears, he heaved a long-suffering sigh that cut into her soul.

"Ciel, I didn't mean—"

"Yes, you did," she replied brokenly. "You warned me all along what we had was only temporary, that it was dangerous and wouldn't—couldn't—work for long, and now—" helplessly, she gestured toward the blazing garage "—I see why."

"It's not just this," he began.

"Yes, I know. I'm not what you need in so many ways, and I can't bear being the ruination of all your dreams." Moisture slid unheeded down her cheeks, and her voice was raw. "So I won't inflict myself on you anymore. When you get home to Houston, you'll find a way to pick up the pieces. I pray that someday you'll also find it in your heart to forgive me for all the trouble I've caused you."

Knowing that if she broke down he'd feel guilty and perhaps say something that would weaken her resolve, she turned away, praying she could reach the house before she shattered completely.

"Ciel, wait—"

The husky timbre of his voice nearly undid her, and she froze, her eyes drifting shut on a wave of pain. She fought the urge to turn and fling herself into his arms. But the responsibility for his loss was hers alone, and she owed him this—the chance to regain his life and his freedom without ties and emotions he'd never asked for complicating the issue. Holding back sobs, she gave him the only answer she could.

"Goodbye, Jack."

And then she ran, slamming through the screened back door of her childhood home, but knowing that the solace she'd always found within it was gone, burned to ashes along with her hopes and her heart in the smoldering ruin of an old garage.

A SINGLE PICKUP TRUCK trundled down Whiskey Bay's deserted Main Street, then turned a corner and disappeared in a blur of red taillights. Ciel unlocked the front door of the *Whiskey Bay Press,* grimacing at her haggard reflection in the window glass, a ghostly image illuminated by the streetlights just buzzing to life in the evening dusk. When you were unemployed, brokenhearted and as tired as a possum treed by a pack of blue tick hounds, looking like a hag wasn't a great consideration.

In fact, after all day dealing with the aftermath of the fire and her breakup with Jack, when she'd finally decided to get to work this evening on the swan song edition of the *Press,* she'd thrown on the first thing she'd found languishing on the dirty-clothes pile on the floor of her closet. Tossing her keys onto the countertop, turning on lights and flipping on the computer, Ciel regretted the choice now—a clingy little floral romper with big pockets that she distinctly remembered Jack unbuttoning with great effect.

"Damn!" Gulping, she threw herself into the computer chair, fighting back a hot prickle of tears.

She had a lead story to write, and this wasn't getting her anywhere. She knew she'd done the right thing, but God, it hurt! How was she going to get through the rest of her life never seeing Jack Cooper again? The thought that he was probably already back in Houston produced a fresh wave of tears, and her nose began to run.

"Oh, hell. Get a grip, Ciel," she muttered, digging in her pockets. She unearthed a peppermint, an unlabeled computer diskette and, thankfully, a tissue.

Sniffling, she wiped her nose and tried to compose herself. Jack might assume that she was some kind of lunatic when it came to mischief and mayhem and flying saucer scares, but she was also a damn good newspaperwoman, and she was going to see that the *Press* went out in style.

First and foremost was to grow up and admit to herself that no extraterrestrials had visited Whiskey Bay. She felt as disappointed as when she'd learned there was no Santa, but a mature adult faced reality. She might not have all the answers, but at least her questions would get some attention. Thinking hard, she began to type her story.

Of course the first thing to report on was Tony and Kyle and their unfortunate pranks. Since Ciel believed them when they claimed they weren't responsible for the first landing site or for a bayou full of dead fish, she couldn't allow their involvement to form a smokescreen around the issue of what was really going on. She couldn't forget Jack's analyses of the fish kill, either.

Then there was Sonny Prejean's threatening to sue Mr. Crenshaw on the basis of the *Press*'s coverage. The fact that Mayor Nabors had taken such delight in Ciel's and the *Press*'s comeuppance was merely icing on the cake, but why had he arbitrarily shut down a lucrative tourist attraction to placate the truck drivers using Ballard Road?

Unless there was something to hide.

Ciel sat back from the keyboard, chewing her lip and frowning. Her earlier despondency was replaced by a growing sense of anger. Dadgumit, but it made her furious when her natural curiosity was thwarted by a bunch of obstructionist windbags! The public had a right to know the truth, and it was Ciel's job—officially employed or not—to discover it. And even if Jack never knew, getting to the bottom of this summer madness would give Ciel a sense of vindication—small consolation when you'd lost the man you loved, but all this Daring Blonde had left.

Ciel's frown grew even darker. Everything kept coming back to Prejean Oil. What exactly was behind all those locked gates? Something had sent Sonny Prejean high enough into orbit to file trespassing charges, when a warning from the sheriff would have sufficed.

Curiosity and determination churned and bubbled, and Ciel's jaw firmed. "Well, *chère,* no time like the present."

Grabbing the diskette she'd found in her pocket, she scribbled "Prejean Oil" on the label, shoved it into the slot on the computer and saved her story.

"I'll show you who's a lunatic, Jack Cooper," she muttered, switching off the machine and office lights and rushing for the door. "This story's going to be a prize-winner—just as soon as I find out how it ends."

HE WAS CRAZY for coming.

He didn't have time for it.

He had nothing to say that would make a hill-of-beans difference.

He also had no choice.

In the gathering dusk, the van's headlights bounced crazily up the Landry driveway, mirroring Jack's turbulent feelings. He had to see Ciel one last time.

The vehicle was loaded with his belongings, along with every experimental beaker of pond scum and scraps of spaghetti-sauce-stained papers and scribbled project notes he'd rescued from the camp's garbage cans. René Ballard, a true friend in need, had arranged for the use of a lab back in Houston starting tonight, staffed with a team of Jack's former students as research volunteers. With the information left in his old office files, there was a chance—a remote one—but still a chance, that given some backbreaking work over the next week or so, Jack might still be able to salvage his grant application, his career and his life.

If he got his rear in gear—pronto.

Which was why it was foolish and counterproductive of him to be wasting time with Ciel Landry. Though he'd be glad to depart from what he'd come to think of as that haunted camp house—haunted by Ciel's sunny presence as much as by the unexplained knocking and the sparkles of swamp gas—a gentleman and a scholar didn't leave without saying goodbye. Though his head told him a clean break was best, the aching emptiness in his heart said he owed her—at the very least—that simple courtesy.

Jack pulled the van to a stop in the drive, then grimaced. Behind the house, standing in the growing twilight near the blackened skeletal remains of the garage, he saw Marie talking with Cleveland Henderson. Ciel's car was gone, a patrol car parked in its usual place.

It had never occurred to Jack that Ciel might not be here, and that only added to his turmoil and confusion.

For a man who prided himself on controlling his emotions, he'd been a mess all day long—tossed by waves of anger, disappointment, loss.

Jack shook his head. It wasn't logical. It was making him crazy. Determinedly, he escorted his wayward emotions to the place where he kept them hidden and under control and slammed the door. It was best this way. Seeing Ciel again wouldn't have solved anything. A word with her mother, and then he'd be on his way back to Houston and the life he'd chosen. And things could finally get back to normal.

When pigs fly the Concorde, Cooper.

As Jack climbed from the van, he had the sneaking suspicion that "normal" was never going to be the same, but he pushed that fear aside and slammed the door on it, too.

"Jack, *cher.*" Marie waved him over. Her hair was mussed and her dark eyes shadowed. Cleveland poked at the charred remains of the garage with a stick, and the musky scent of smoke and burning still lay heavily on the sultry twilight air. "I'm glad you're here."

"Can't stay, Marie. I'm headed for Houston this minute to reconstruct my project. Ciel's not here? I wanted—" Jack broke off as something in her expression snagged his attention. "What's wrong?"

"Cleveland says it was arson."

"What?"

"Yes, sir," the deputy said, pointing. "See the direction of that burn? It was set, all right."

"But who, why—? Where's Ciel?"

"She went down to the newspaper office."

Jack's stomach lurched with pure fear. "Alone? This late?"

"She said she had work to do." Staring at the ruined

garage, Marie bit her lip. "I never worried before, but the place was vandalized, and now this...."

"I'll go after her." Jaw clenched, Jack jogged for the van.

"But you're going to Houston," Marie called after him. "What about your project?"

What about it? There would be other projects, other opportunities. But there was only one Ciel, one woman whose special sunshine illuminated every corner of his soul, and someone was trying to hurt her. Nothing was more important than keeping her safe. Nothing was more important than Ciel herself.

His hand poised over the van's door handle, Jack faltered, stunned. *Good God, I love her.*

But was it too late? He'd held back from it first, too cowardly to risk himself, while Ciel with her enthusiasm for life and effervescent joy had been courageous and honest, openly confessing her feelings for him. He might have soared on blazing rockets into space, but that was nothing compared with the courage of this feisty, loving woman who'd given him everything she had—body, heart, soul.

Only, he'd been too craven to accept that wonderful gift.

Shame scorched him. So he was a man who didn't trust emotion. What had that gotten him? Nothing but loneliness and isolation. But did he possess the nerve to trust his feelings now? To risk it all—his fears, his dreams, the very essence of himself—for her sake? And even if he could, what arrogance to think she might still want him—selfish, withholding bastard that he was.

Swallowing hard, Jack knew that he really had no choice, not if his life was ever to have any meaning. He had to find Ciel, and he had to tell her the truth, that he loved her and needed her beyond telling.

So she believed in alien visitors. So what? A beginning of a smile touched his lips. What the hell, it was a possibility. She also believed in life and hope and maybe even Jack Cooper. And perhaps, if he was lucky, he could find a place in Ciel's life. He only knew he had to try, and nothing else was important.

"Jack? *Cher,* you best get on the highway if you're going to Houston," Marie was saying. "I'll go find that daughter of mine, don't you worry. So get on home. We all know what that project means to you."

Jack climbed into the van and took a giant leap that would have made Neil Armstrong proud.

"It'll keep."

CROUCHED BEHIND a palmetto fan, within shooting distance of the main gates, Ciel gripped her flashlight and let out a low whistle of disbelief. For a facility that should have been quiet and dark and deserted well after business hours, Prejean Oil and Engineering was up and running full steam ahead.

Floodlights illuminated the dust-choked compound. A steady stream of tankers, eighteen-wheelers and dump trucks rolled in the open gates empty, and exited loaded to the hilt. Forklifts and backhoes scurried back and forth, heaping vehicles with wooden pallets stacked with iron drums. Laborers in hard hats sweated on the loading docks, grunting and swearing as they moved siphon hoses as thick as elephant trunks from barrels to tankers. The whole operation had an air of suppressed urgency about it that confirmed Ciel's suspicions. There *was* something going on at Prejean Oil!

Only, how to discover exactly what? And how to do it without getting caught herself?

Well, Sylvie Fairstar wouldn't be faint of heart. Ciel drew a deep breath, cranked up her courage, then, using a cloud of dust from a passing eighteen-wheeler as a screen, darted inside the compound. Retracing her earlier course toward the locked gate at the rear, she sprinted through the shadows around the towers of barrels, their numbers now mysteriously depleted by the feverish activity. Either Prejean Oil was doing an exceptional amount of business, or someone was trying to remove evidence. But evidence of what?

Thankfully, all the activity seemed to be taking place in the main compound. Ciel peered around a pallet to be sure no one was looking her way before she made her move. An old tanker that looked as if it had been wrecked more than once idled at the loading dock. Fluid dripped from the rear of its battered, rusty tank, seeping into the dry earth to form a giant bruise. Something niggled at Ciel's memory, but then a shout made her duck back behind the pallet, her heart pounding.

After a few tense moments, when no one appeared, she let go of the breath she didn't even know she'd been holding. With a final look to all sides, she made a break for the gate with its ominous warning sign, finding to her relief that the padlocks hung loose. Slipping through the opening, she thumbed her flashlight, then gasped.

Before her was a nightmare vision of tortured metal superstructures, leaking tanks, oozing puddles of noxious, evil-smelling sludge that trickled in a steamy stream underneath the back fence. Around the perimeter, what vegetation there was sported seared leaves and twisted, mutated stems. Pointing the flash, Ciel picked out key words on drum labels: *Danger. Toxic. Environ-*

mental Hazard. Warning. Poison. All that was needed to complete the picture was a monster—and Ciel was suddenly sure his name was Sonny Prejean and he'd been poisoning Whiskey Bay!

She wished fervently that Jack were there. He'd know what it all meant much better than she could, but she'd bet her last nickel that Sonny's waste management policies left much to be desired and that all the dead fish and dead rice and mutated plants and overgrown animals could be traced to this shoddy, obviously illegal operation. And if she could reveal it and give Jack credit for his help, maybe that would make up for some of the damage she'd done his reputation and career!

With a final look and a shudder of revulsion, she backed toward the gate. A hand came out of nowhere, chopping her wrist. Ciel yelped and dropped the flashlight. A meaty fist knotted in the back of her jumper, swinging her around half off her feet. Sonny Prejean's screech split the air.

"Oh, no! Not you again!"

"CIEL? SUNSHINE, are you in there?"

Jack squinted through the newspaper office's darkened window, his heart sinking at the lack of activity. Where was the woman? Frustrated, he knocked on the casing and rattled the doorknob. The door swung open.

Rushing inside, he fumbled for the light switches, calling her name, his imagination working overtime, dreading what he might find. A quick inspection proved the office was as empty as it seemed, and relieved him of all but his greatest worry—where the hell was she? With Ciel's impetuosity, there was no guessing. But with some nameless, faceless threat out there, he had to catch up with her—fast.

Marie said Ciel had come to work on her story. Jack's gaze went to the dark computer. Maybe that would shed some light. Bending over the keyboard, he turned on the machine, then noticed the black plastic diskette labeled "Prejean Oil" in the slot.

"Bingo!" he muttered.

Tapping rapidly, he accessed the list of file names stored on the disk. He blinked, then gave a bark of incredulous laughter. There was her story, all right—along with files containing not only her Sylvie Fairstar chapters but his very own project data, dated just days earlier! While that file wouldn't contain his final analyses, it was his grant proposal, largely intact!

"Ciel, you redheaded wonder! How on earth did you do this?"

Images of scrambled documents and diskettes flung across an office and a certain close encounter on a day-bed spilled into Jack's head. He grinned. God, the woman had the luck of the Irish in her Cajun blood, and she'd probably saved his skin, career-wise, with that klutzy incident, but none of that was as important as finding her now. Ignoring his work, he pulled up her story file.

But as he read her notes, his expression darkened, and a new fear consumed him. All her speculations and conjectures made perfect sense, but was she loony enough to think she could take on Prejean by herself?

Think like Ciel, Jack instructed himself, then gulped. Of course she'd try to tackle the bad guys singlehandedly just like Sylvie Fairstar! That was just her style. And if Sonny Prejean was desperate enough to resort to arson, then Ciel could be in a pile of trouble.

Jack bolted for the door, muttering, "So what else is new?"

THE BULKY security guard hauled Ciel after Sonny Prejean into the shadows behind a dilapidated tractor-trailer rig.

"What the hell's *she* doing here?"

"Snooping—what'd ya think?" Sonny snapped, temper puffing his barrel chest under his cowboy shirt.

Ciel raised a hand to shield her eyes from the guard's flashlight, recognizing the newcomer with a shock. "Emile!"

She blinked dizzily, then everything clicked into place and she hit the jackpot.

"The city contracts! And the landfill lease on city land. You've been letting Sonny get away with murder for a price, haven't you, Emile?" she accused hotly, trying to shrug off her captor's restraining hand. "What's he paying you?"

"Oh, hell, now you've really done it," the mayor of Whiskey Bay complained. "She's onto us, bubba."

"Shut up, Emile, and let me think."

"Should have known messin' up her office and rattling old Crenshaw's cage wouldn't slow her down."

"Well, she ain't got proof anymore, right?" Sonny growled. "A can of kerosene saw to that. And I'll have everything else shipped out of here by dawn, so just relax. Go count that retirement fund I've contributed to so often and so generously and quit yer griping."

Ciel's eyes widened. "Wait a minute! Kerosene? You mean you burned down my mama's garage? You dirty, lowdown—"

She kicked out, catching Sonny on the kneecap. He yowled and grabbed his leg, hopping up and down on one cowboy-booted foot.

"You idjit female—you damn near broke my knee!"

Twisting, feinting at him with her fists, Ciel snarled

back, "I'd like to break your neck, you lowlife scumbag! And yours, too, *Mayor*."

Emile *tsked*, gloating at her predicament. "Such violence from a lady. What's the world coming to?"

"When I tell the world what's been going on out here, they're going to put you both *under* the jail!"

"That tears it!" Sonny's face contorted. "Toss her inside, Hurkey."

Wordlessly, the guard dragged Ciel to the open rear doors of the big trailer, lifted her as easily as a rag doll and shoved her in among the stacks of barrels filling the rig. Tumbling, Ciel landed on her side with a *whuff*, then scrambled to her skinned knees, wheezing. "You can't do this!"

"This rig's headed for an unregulated landfill in Mexico," Sonny chortled. "By the time anyone finds you, we'll be long gone. *Adios*."

"I hear the weather's splendid this time of year in Tahiti," Emile remarked.

Alarm raced through Ciel's veins, and she surged to her feet. "Hey, wait! You can't—"

The doors slammed shut, plunging Ciel into total darkness.

"Hey!" Feeling her way to the rear, she pounded on the doors with her fists, hollering at the top of her lungs. Then the floor jerked out from under her, toppling her to her bottom as the old truck lurched, changed gears, lurched again and began to pick up speed. "Oh, God!"

An adventure in Mexico might have a certain appeal in other circumstances, but Ciel didn't relish this particular mode of transportation. The trailer swayed violently, making the loaded barrels groan and screech in protest. Ciel hugged the smelly, half-rotten floor in the darkness and tried not to think about being crushed or dehydration or any number of other evils.

Think! Think like Jack, she ordered herself. What would the logical professor do in a situation like this?

The hiss of air brakes, a sharp turn—Ciel flattened herself against the bed of the trailer again. The faint reddish glow of the brake lights filtered through the cracked floorboards, illuminating a tangle of loose wiring coiling like snakes. With a flare of sudden, desperate inspiration, she went to work.

GRIM-LIPPED, Jack floored the accelerator and his old van tore down Ballard Road like an Atlas booster at full burn. There was no doubt in his mind that Ciel was at this very moment at Prejean Oil, and when he got his hands on her, he was either going to kiss her senseless or wring her freckled neck!

Preoccupied with the image, he nearly didn't see the eighteen-wheeler when it roared from behind a moss-draped oak and took the curve in the middle of the narrow road. Swearing, horn blaring, Jack swerved onto the shoulder, narrowly missing the rig as it blasted past with a Doppler scream of air horns and a blur of blinking lights.

Drenched in sweat, cursing, Jack eased off the accelerator and steered the bucking van back onto the road. He glared into the rearview mirror at the truck's retreating taillights, then frowned. The driver obviously had a short in his electrical system that was producing a series of curiously rhythmic flashes.

On, off, on, off, on, off. On—on—on.

Short, short, short. Long, long, long. Short, short—

Jack stood on his brakes so hard the van fishtailed and all the bottles of algae loaded in the boxes behind his seat clattered in protest. Wrenching the wheel back under control, he swung around in his seat, eyes narrowed on the rapidly disappearing truck.

What *was* it? Realization slammed into him like a jackhammer. Dot, dot, dot—dash, dash, dash—dot, dot, dot!

S-O-S! Morse code. *Ciel!* He knew it in his gut, in his heart. Instinct warred with logic, and for once in his life he trusted what he could only feel. It had to be!

Reversing, Jack spun the van around and raced after the truck, blinking his lights, blowing his horn. He caught up with the rig half a mile onto the main highway, but the driver ignored his signals. In fact, he picked up speed as he raced through Whiskey Bay's deserted streets.

And still those taillights flashed—on, off, on, off. Were they getting slower now? Was she tiring? Hurt? Jack's chest felt as though it would explode. He had to stop that truck somehow!

Up ahead, on the outskirts of town, Jack spotted the neon ice-cream-cone sign shining over the Snow-Breez Drive-In, the only lively spot in town since the demise of the landing site. Reaching behind the seat, he grabbed a box of algae samples, slowed the van slightly, then, with only faint regret, hefted six bottles one right after the other onto the asphalt in front of the Snow-Breez.

They hit with the sound of small bombs exploding, spewing green goo in all directions. Kids scrambled, girls gave startled screams and one observant young man pointed and shouted, "Look, it's the spaceman!"

"Call the cops!" Jack roared out the window, then hit the gas again.

This time, when he caught up with the truck he didn't waste time trying to flag it down, just punched the accelerator and passed it, praying that the van's laboring engine wouldn't explode and that the deserted highway would stay that way.

From far away, he heard the first faint wails of sirens and grinned. This wouldn't do his reputation any good, and he'd probably end up in jail again, but he didn't give a damn. All that mattered was Ciel.

Pulling up ahead of the speeding rig, he lobbed vials out the window. They splattered behind him on the highway, scattering shards of glass and pea-green liquid in the path of the eighteen-wheeler. The truck dodged, swerved, braked, skidded—and with a screech of air brakes slid off the road into the shallow ditch and came to a shuddering halt.

Jack slammed on brakes, reversed until he came even with the rig, then vaulted out of the van, holding a beaker aloft in each hand with menacing intent. The bulky driver wore a blue security guard's uniform, and he hurled himself out of the cab of the truck at Jack.

"You crazy SOB! I ought to—"

Jack lifted the vial. "Get down! This is plague virus and I swear I'll use it!"

"Plague?" Blanching, the big man dropped onto his rotund belly, hands upraised in surrender. "Sure, mister, anything you say."

Twin patrol cars barreled up the highway behind them, red lights rotating, sirens screaming.

Dropping the vials in the ditch, Jack charged to the rear of the trailer and threw open the doors. A red-haired figure sprawled on the floor, groaning. Jack dragged her into his arms, running his hands over her for injuries, trying to see into her face.

"Ciel! Sunshine, are you all right?"

"Jack?" Her arms fastened around his neck in a stranglehold. "Oh, Jack!"

"Easy, sunshine, I'm here," he murmured, kissing her. "And I'm never leaving orbit without you again."

Patrolmen swarmed them, guns drawn, speaking into walkie-talkies. One ordered the driver to his feet. Another shone a flashlight into the trailer, gave a startled look and waved to a companion to come see. Jack ignored them and kissed her again.

"Jack," she gasped when he lifted his head, "it's Sonny. He and Emile, pouring all sorts of contaminated wastes into the landfill. It killed those fish, and I'll bet that old tanker broke down and leaked its load into the rice field."

"You mean it really wasn't Martians?" Jack asked in mock horror. "Oh, damn!"

"Jack, be serious! They're getting away. Something about Tahiti—"

"We'll sic the cops on them, sunshine. They won't get far."

"They were sending me to Mexico," she wailed. "I didn't want to go."

"I don't blame you. Mexico's got no pizzazz these days. I'll take you to the rain forest for our honeymoon."

"Huh?"

He pressed a kiss to her temple. "Think you could write science fiction sitting around a campsite in Brazil with your husband? Say yes, and I'll dance the *lambada* at our wedding."

Ciel drew back, her eyes like saucers. "What are you talking about?"

"I'm trying to say—" He took an unsteady breath. "I'm crazy in love with you, sunshine. It took me a while to figure it out, but I'm not worth a damn without you. If you still love me and can forgive me for being such a blockhead, I think maybe we ought to get married, don't you?''

She brushed back her flyaway curls with shaky fingers and gave him a stern look. "Don't make jokes, Professor. I've had a bad day."

He cupped her face between his palms. "I've never been more serious about anything in my life."

"Oh."

"Is that a yes?"

Her smile was as slow and radiant as a new dawn. "Yes."

"Good, I'm glad we've got that settled." He grinned at her and nodded toward the advancing cordon of patrol officers. "We're going to be explaining all this for quite a while. Feel up to spending a night in jail with me?"

"Anywhere you want."

He growled. "I like the sound of that."

Laughing softly, blushing, she snuggled under his protective arm. "How'd you know I was inside the truck?"

"Easy. I just looked where chaos reigned and there you were."

"Thanks." Dryly.

"The Morse code helped, though," he admitted. "You're something, Daring Blonde. I love you."

"Me, too, Professor—and after what you've done tonight, I dare anyone to call you dull ever again!" She looked down at the splattered ooze at her feet. "What's all this—" She broke off with a gasp. "Jack! Not your algae samples."

"I had to use them to stop that truck."

"They're all broken? Oh, no, your project! Now I've ruined everything again! How—"

He stopped her wails with another fiery kiss, murmuring against her lips. "Relax, sunshine, you're worth more to me than an ocean of algae."

"Oh, Jack, what a lovely thing to say. You're sure?" She looked doubtful, hopeful, relieved.

"Absolutely. Besides, I've got a few things to tell you, too—all good."

"I can't wait." She giggled. "You know, it's not every girl who can say her guy rode to her rescue on a vat of pond scum!"

He shrugged, grinning. "That's me, 'Pond Scum 'R Us.'"

"I know," she said, laughing, "it's your life."

Jack shook his head, his expression tender, his voice husky with love. "No, sunshine. You are."

Epilogue

"ELVIS, is that you?"

Rousing from a catnap, Etienne Ballard raised his grizzled head, listening. Only the barest whisper stirred the purple twilight at the Harbor Home Retirement Center. With a sigh, he set his rocking chair in motion again and selected a caramel-filled chocolate from the enormous box on the table beside him. A copy of the *Whiskey Bay Press* sat beside the box.

Etienne scanned the headlines.

Paper Changes Hands. Lauren And Tiny Herbert New Editors.

Marie Landry Announces Candidacy For Mayor.

Nabors And Prejean Indicted, EPA Vows Complete Cleanup.

Chamber Plans "I Was Hoaxed" UFO Festival For Next Year.

Etienne took a bite of candy, savoring the sweetness.

"Awfully nice of those kids to remember an old man," he said conversationally to the empty porch. "Especially what with all the excitement about Ciel's selling her novel and then them heading off on their honeymoon to Brazil. That Jack must be a smart fellow, getting all that money to study pond scum."

He cocked his head, listening expectantly, then continued.

"You boys ever been to Brazil, Elvis? No, I 'spect

not. Best little vacation spot on the planet right here. Got a little carried away this year, though, didn't you?" Etienne cackled with laughter. "Shake, rattle and roll. Gets 'em every time!"

"Mr. Ballard, time to come in." A white-uniformed nurse appeared at Etienne's side. She cupped his elbow, helping him to his feet, a puzzled expression on her face. "You talking to someone?"

"Just a couple of very old, very dear friends of mine, Warden."

The nurse's smile was indulgent. "I see. Oh, no—candy! Mr. Ballard, you shouldn't!"

He winked, picked up the box, then offered her his arm. "Don't tell, and I'll give you the whiskey-filled ones."

"Mr. Ballard, you are a scandal!" Walking slowly, they moved toward the entrance door. "Well, maybe just one...."

FINE GENTLEMAN

AND A GOOD HOST

PROVIDED EXCELLENT ENTERTAINMENT THIS YEAR

YES, BUT I'LL NEVER UNDERSTAND EARTHLINGS, COSMO

ME, NEITHER, ELVIS. LET'S GO HOME

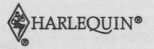

Happy
Birthday to

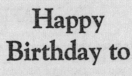

It's party time....
This year is our
40th anniversary!

**Forty years of
bringing you the best
in romance fiction—and
the best just keeps
getting better!**

To celebrate, we're planning
three months of fun, and prizes.

Not to mention, of course,
some fabulous books...

The party starts in **April** with:

Betty Neels
Emma Richmond
Kate Denton
Barbara McMahon

Come join the party!

HARLEQUIN®

Don't miss these Harlequin favorites by some of our most distinguished authors!
And now, you can receive a discount by ordering two or more titles!

HT#25645	THREE GROOMS AND A WIFE by JoAnn Ross	$3.25 U.S. $3.75 CAN.	☐
HT#25647	NOT THIS GUY by Glenda Sanders	$3.25 U.S. $3.75 CAN.	☐
HP#11725	THE WRONG KIND OF WIFE by Roberta Leigh	$3.25 U.S. $3.75 CAN.	☐
HP#11755	TIGER EYES by Robyn Donald	$3.25 U.S. $3.75 CAN.	☐
HR#03416	A WIFE IN WAITING by Jessica Steele	$3.25 U.S. $3.75 CAN.	☐
HR#03419	KIT AND THE COWBOY by Rebecca Winters	$3.25 U.S. $3.75 CAN.	☐
HS#70622	KIM & THE COWBOY by Margot Dalton	$3.50 U.S. $3.99 CAN.	☐
HS#70642	MONDAY'S CHILD by Janice Kaiser	$3.75 U.S. $4.25 CAN.	☐
HI#22342	BABY VS. THE BAR by M.J. Rodgers	$3.50 U.S. $3.99 CAN.	☐
HI#22382	SEE ME IN YOUR DREAMS by Patricia Rosemoor	$3.75 U.S. $4.25 CAN.	☐
HAR#16538	KISSED BY THE SEA by Rebecca Flanders	$3.50 U.S. $3.99 CAN.	☐
HAR#16603	MOMMY ON BOARD by Muriel Jensen	$3.50 U.S. $3.99 CAN.	☐
HH#28885	DESERT ROGUE by Erine Yorke	$4.50 U.S. $4.99 CAN.	☐
HH#28911	THE NORMAN'S HEART by Margaret Moore	$4.50 U.S. $4.99 CAN.	☐

(limited quantities available on certain titles)

	AMOUNT	$
DEDUCT:	**10% DISCOUNT FOR 2+ BOOKS**	$
ADD:	**POSTAGE & HANDLING**	$
	($1.00 for one book, 50¢ for each additional)	
	APPLICABLE TAXES*	$_____
	TOTAL PAYABLE	$_____
	(check or money order—please do not send cash)	

To order, complete this form and send it, along with a check or money order for the total above, payable to Harlequin Books, to: **In the U.S.:** 3010 Walden Avenue, P.O. Box 9047, Buffalo, NY 14269-9047; **In Canada:** P.O. Box 613, Fort Erie, Ontario, L2A 5X3.

Name:_____

Address:_____ City:_____

State/Prov.:_____ Zip/Postal Code:_____

*New York residents remit applicable sales taxes.
 Canadian residents remit applicable GST and provincial taxes.
Look us up on-line at: http://www.romance.net

HBACK-JM4

This March, Harlequin brings you
a wonderful collection of
stories celebrating family, in...

YOURS, MINE

& *Ours*

Written by three of your favorite authors

PENNY JORDAN
CATHY GILLEN THACKER
MARISA CARROLL

How do two families become one? Just add love!
Available anywhere Harlequin books are sold.

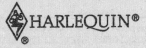

HARLEQUIN®

Free Gift Offer

With a Free Gift proof-of-purchase
from any Harlequin® book, you can receive
a beautiful cubic zirconia pendant.

This stunning marquise-shaped stone is a genuine cubic
zirconia—accented by an 18" gold tone necklace.
(Approximate retail value $19.95)

Send for yours today...
compliments of ◈HARLEQUIN®

To receive your free gift, a cubic zirconia pendant, send us one original proof-of-purchase, photocopies not accepted, from the back of any Harlequin Romance®, Harlequin Presents®, Harlequin Temptation®, Harlequin Superromance®, Harlequin Intrigue®, Harlequin American Romance®, or Harlequin Historicals® title available in February, March or April at your favorite retail outlet, together with the Free Gift Certificate, plus a check or money order for $1.65 U.S./$2.15 CAN. (do not send cash) to cover postage and handling, payable to Harlequin Free Gift Offer. We will send you the specified gift. Allow 6 to 8 weeks for delivery. Offer good until April 30, 1997, or while quantities last. Offer valid in the U.S. and Canada only.

Free Gift Certificate

Name: _____

Address: _____

City: _____ State/Province: _____ Zip/Postal Code: _____

Mail this certificate, one proof-of-purchase and a check or money order for postage and handling to: HARLEQUIN FREE GIFT OFFER 1997. In the U.S.: 3010 Walden Avenue, P.O. Box 9071, Buffalo NY 14269-9057. In Canada: P.O. Box 604, Fort Erie, Ontario L2Z 5X3.

FREE GIFT OFFER   084-KEZ

ONE PROOF-OF-PURCHASE

To collect your fabulous FREE GIFT, a cubic zirconia pendant, you must include this
original proof-of-purchase for each gift with the properly completed Free Gift Certificate.

084-KEZ

Heartbreak RANCH

Four generations of independent women...
Four heartwarming, romantic stories of the West...
Four incredible authors...

Fern Michaels
Jill Marie Landis
Dorsey Kelley
Chelley Kitzmiller

Saddle up with Heartbreak Ranch, an outstanding
Western collection that will take you on a whirlwind
trip through four generations and the exciting,
romantic adventures of four strong women who
have inherited the ranch from Bella Duprey,
famed Barbary Coast madam.

Available in March,
wherever Harlequin books are sold.

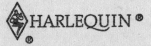

HARLEQUIN ®

You're About to Become a

Privileged Woman

Reap the rewards of fabulous free gifts and benefits with proofs-of-purchase from Harlequin and Silhouette books

Pages & Privileges™

It's our way of thanking you for buying our books at your favorite retail stores.

PROOF OF PURCHASE LL-PP23

Offer expires March 31, 1997

Pages & Privileges ™

**Harlequin and Silhouette—
the most privileged readers in the world!**

For more information about Harlequin and Silhouette's PAGES & PRIVILEGES program call the Pages & Privileges Benefits Desk: 1-503-794-2499

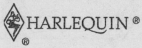

HARLEQUIN ®

LL-PP23